THE

HIDDEN

GENRE

Also by Michael de Oliveira

C.H.H. AIN'T DEAD

The Hidden Genre

C. H. H. AIN'T DEAD: THE HIDDEN GENRE

MICHAEL DE OLIVEIRA

To Elohim, the Most High, be the glory!
This is dedicated to those representing Him
In the entertainment industry.

To my step pops, you will forever live in our
hearts.

PROLOGUE

WHO WON?

When chairs creaked in the silence that overcame the arena, the MC glared at the crowd as if they were to reveal the answer. All eyes were glued to the stage, glued to the TV screen, glued to the envelope in the MC's hand. He held one name inside it and it had more attention than the two rappers on each side awaiting their destiny.

The winner would be given a contract by Decep Records.

The loser would be given a handshake by misery herself.

They both dreamed of making it, but faced the hard truth that only one of them would get to live it out.

The judges' eyes were stone cold. No facial muscles twitched. They knew who the winner was, but had no intentions of giving any hints away. It didn't matter. The crowd weren't searching for any. Each had their own opinion of who won.

DJ Smacks kept everyone on the edge of suspense, while the MC gave the contestants one more glance, but their eyes were firmly on the crowd as he slowly revealed the name to himself.

Were they not friends? These two rappers . . . if they didn't show any signs of knowing one another now. How much more so when one was touring the world, while the other toured the daily nine to five routine of life?

"And the winner is . . ." the MC's face expression sparked murmurs amongst the crowd.

Was it a draw? And if that was the case, would the record label give contracts to both finalists? Or was he completely surprised at this year's winner?

"Luke Chase . . ."

"Give it up for this year's winner, Luke Chase!" DJ Smacks echoed over the shockwave that hit the crowd.

The rapper to the MC's left had a huge cloud burst of movement! Complete opposite to the amount of energy used in the MC's announcement. Winning this competition meant Luke clearly had the talent to go far in the industry, but the same couldn't be said about his dancing. Nevertheless, the vibe was contagious and like a virus the cheers spread throughout the arena.

The shock of the words that left the MC's mouth was so intense that the protocol of comforting the loser almost slipped his mind. He turned only to see that the loser had faded backstage already. His kid walked away with the world on his shoulders as tears were streaming down his face.

The MC's body temperature rose and made him light headed; as sight became a magnified mirror. He blew his cheeks as if the heat would exit his mouth like what his kid spat. The noise of the crowd blurred out like everyone else around him. Only his wife sprinting towards her son was within his sight. He couldn't process the fact that he was forced to announce that his kid lost the battle, especially when it felt to be the complete opposite.

"Don't let it get to you, son," he heard his wife say. "Sometimes the words mean more once understanding is possible."

Had the judges got it wrong, or was this *just* a parent thing?

THE HIDDEN GENRE

"Welcome to Decep Records, Luke Chase," the agent pulled up on stage with a smile that one would normally see on a proud father. "Now, let's conquer the world!"

THE HIDDEN GENRE

THREE
YEARS
LATER

THE HIDDEN GENRE

ONE

MORNING CAME too soon for the young man drooling over his papers. It was a slow and silent waterfall which made the ink spread out like it tried to escape the inevitable. The word *world* was the center and it spread throughout the pages like streams. If he went by the name, Noah, it would've been a clear sign of the future. But this wasn't the case, and this wasn't a story about a flood wiping the mainstream clean. This unknown person was known to many as the Gospel Rapper, not Isaac Banner.

"Son, are you ready to leave? You're going to be late –" Mrs. Banner broke into the room to witness what most parents do. "You are going to be *very* late actually."

She pulled out her smartphone and its screen got excited seeing her face. She found the contact titled, Isaac, without the need to wake him up, until Mrs. Banner "accidentally" pressed the green button and put the phone to her ear like the good old days.

Glad they didn't change that . . .

"I'm screaming, Jesus! Jesus! Jesus! Till my eyes close!" yelled the object next to her son's head.

Isaac shot up. He immediately grabbed the phone and wiped his face without the slightest awareness of his surroundings. The technology got no side eye for waking him up, yet Mrs. Banner swore she's been given the eyes many times in the past as he answered, "Hello?"

"You're late," she said. Her son turned slightly and gave her side eye, "if you're going to wake up this quick when you hear *that* song. Why don't you set it as your alarm?"

Isaac put the smartphone next to his pages. "Come on, mom," he gave them a quick glance as if wondering how they got wet. "You know I'm waiting for one of these record labels to get back to me. Hearing that song makes me think God is finally about to put me on that path."

"So? Me phoning may mean just that," replied Mrs. Banner, but she received a "*like really* mom" glance from her son. Motherly, she had a point. Logically, she didn't.

"Son, if you meant to preach on the mainstream, then it's only perfect timing that's delaying it," said his mom, trying to comfort her son, "just keep trusting that your time will come."

"I know, mom. It's just . . . it just hasn't been the same ever since . . . well, you know . . ." Isaac stopped mid-way through his sentence.

Mrs. Banner watched her son's head drop. She understood. But she wasn't going to add to his energy, "I told Chantal that you're going to be late today. I mentioned that you were burning the midnight oil with a new song and she said that Ruth did the same thing last night."

"Wait, Mrs. Rennells *actually* used her name?" Isaac asked.

"Not really, but don't you want to find out what she wrote?" added Mrs. Banner, "maybe Cupid made you two write lyrics that would only make sense when they came together. When you guys finally come together."

That got no reply, but a much needed smile.

"Here," his mom tossed him a towel hanging from behind the door. It didn't make it, but it sure forced Isaac to stretch and fall into the heap of dirty clothing. "I think you need to go shower before we leave," she gave herself an excuse to ask the question, "haven't I told you that cleanliness is next to godliness?"

"Yes, you have, mom," he replied, "and I've mentioned many times that it's not in the scriptures."

"Oh," she got comfortable on her son's chair. "Then have I mentioned the verse about Jesus washing the disciples' feet?"

+++

It was not long before they were on the road and stuck in traffic. That was more surprising than the good boy's immediate burst towards the shower to avoid his mom's feet. On a normal day, the cars would have reached their destination by this time in the morning, but not today. Today they bunched up like ants preparing to accept their queen. However, this queen was a horrific accident.

"Yes, mam, you heard right," the cop on duty said, "the scene of the accident is not what you would want a youngster to see."

Mrs. Banner's son shifted his headphones and laid back. He must have let the darkness consume him to avoid hearing or seeing what the officer informed them about.

"It's fine, he's 22," she tried to make it convincing, but it wasn't working as much as it was true. Even if Isaac took his identification card with him to a club, the bouncer would think it was a fake - maybe another teenager trying to have an under aged experience.

"Look, mam, all I'm saying is that it can be very traumatizing, but you can rest assure that we doing the best we can," the cop convinced himself more than the civilian.

"I understand, but can you at least say what happened? I may not look it, but I'm a citizen of Amboria too. And I know my rights. I know I have the right to know what's happening so close to home," insisted Mrs. Banner.

"Actually -" began the cop.

"The NCPA have been shooting people recently -" Mrs. Banner interjected.

"No, mam, please remain calm, it wasn't a shootout," replied the cop, very quickly, as if to not create any panic.

"I'm very much calm, officer . . ." Mrs. Banner took a quick glance at his name badge, "Den." If she had any doubt that this officer wasn't in training, recognizing the surname and not his first name, was the final nail in the coffin. "I just need to decide if my son, who has huge dreams, is safe being guided by the cops," she quickly added, "that's all . . ."

"Okay, jeez, please cut me some slack, mam, it's my first day out the academy," said the cop, visibly tired.

"Oh, I'm sorry, where's my manners?" asked Mrs. Banner, not expecting an answer, "congrats on your achievement Officer Den."

"Dave," he replied with a smile. "You can call me, Dave."

"Are you related to an Oscar Den by any chance?" asked Mrs. Banner.

"Yes, he's my father," replied Officer Den with a smile.

"Ah, I see it now. I think you'll make your father proud, Dave," said Mrs. Banner, complimenting him.

"Thank you very much, mam."

Isaac moved his head towards his window and opened his eyes. His eyes found the bright ocean sky. Clouds were scattered all round like social groups in high school. The biggest group's edges were carved out to portray a face. The face of the man he hadn't seen in three years. The man, he himself, tried to make proud.

"Is he okay?" asked the officer, noticing the boy's sudden amazement with the sky.

"Don't worry about him," she replied, "he's late for work, but too polite to tell us to stop talking and hurry up."

"Stop talking and hurry up!" came a voice from behind them with a couple of hoots, "some of us are late for work!"

"All we can say right now, mam: is that a truck lost control and basically rammed everything in its way," said Officer Den quickly, "my advice is to take the detour but as you can see, I'm being ignored. One driver even told me that she's going to be *too* late if she takes the detour; plus she's seen horror movies before, so -"

The car ahead moved forward and turned the stereo up as if the driver got tired of hearing the cop's voice. Traffic moved as a whole.

"You have to go now, mam, but be sure to listen to the radio for updates," said the officer, sending them off.

Mrs. Banner put the officer's words into motion. The detour path was narrow, but spacious and uphill.

+++

16

THE HIDDEN GENRE

The road guided the uphill goers straight into the light. Isaac tried to avoid the rays as they took the turn, but that inch of a second was all the sun needed to leave a temporal flash of colours.

Had he heard everything the officer said? When he touched his headphones, did Isaac change the song, or pause the music? Mrs. Banner knew her son, he stole much of his information without the knowledge of those speaking. However . . . he couldn't handle accidents. He couldn't handle *that* pain. He couldn't handle *that* death, yet.

News channels that reported the amount of fatalities in accidents, never mention how each came to be. But Isaac always understood why . . . yet that never stopped the thoughts from plaguing his mind:

What if the person didn't die instantly? How does it feel as you lie there, knowingly sinking into the arms of death? Who do you think of during that moment? Do you think about the pain your death will cause your loved ones? Do you think about life after? Or do you think about how you can't complete your plans for the day? Your plans for the future? Whether or not you'll return as a newborn baby?

These thoughts infested his brain. Not the gore. But the realization that that's that. Your life was about to end as unexpectedly as it started. Regardless, Isaac had no reason to fear death.

"It actually copied your room by the sound of it," Mrs. Banner tried to get her son to lighten up, "it was messy."

She got a struggled grin. Yes, the joke was inappropriate, especially since . . .

The main point was: she cracked the case of whether Isaac's music was paused or not.

Now what? He didn't make any attempts to press play on his headphones. Maybe he wanted to listen to some of his mother's rock music. Some Skillet? No, some Spoken? Neither . . . Isaac was more into rap than rock, unlike her. A bit of both worlds with some Trevor McNevan and Manafest perhaps? No, that was more his father's type of music. And it won't help thinking about *him* right now, especially since . . .

Maybe turning on the radio would be the best option. No. She knew the radio was the best option. Isaac would normally put his headphones on and drown in the lyrics. Today was different.

The radio grunted like it wasn't ready to wake up.

"Welcome - to the - show," a voice on the North City Radio came alive. "Our guests today are DJ Johnny and C:map. Two upcoming *Christian* artists."

Isaac's head snapped towards the radio. Yes, the woman's voice was smooth and gentle, and yes, men could probably listen to it whole day. But that was not what grabbed her son's attention . . . right?

The woman continued, "First up, the man behind the scenes, DJ Johnny. His instrumentals are currently taking the industry by storm. Tell me, why did you choose to work with C:map when you had many other secular options?"

"The answer goes way back, Tammy. He and I went to high school together. He popped by *uninvited* and caught me in the middle of making beats. I usually create on my off days, so his timing was spot on. Then, randomly he just started spitting flames. I thought he gave up, since he stopped for a year or so, you know."

"I see -" said Tammy, doing her job of sounding like the interested interviewer.

"I see it more as: one whole year of learning," added C:map, "I couldn't get rusty since I studied the Word of God."

"But everyone that has heard your previous music, knows that you are considered a secular artist," said Tammy, "what I'm really trying to get at, is this: are you now a rapper that is Christian, or a Christian rapper?"

There was a slight pause. For he knew the answer, but he needed to use this opportunity to say it correctly, "I'm going to answer that now, but first, you know what I find amusing? Many of these Christian artists want to separate themselves from other "Christians," but not from other rappers."

"I see, like the difference between a *set apart one* and a *Sunday Christian?* That's a big statement to make though," said Tammy.

"I know there's this debate on who's what, and who's both," DJ Johnny got involved, "but from what we believe, we are not of this world."

"Well said, Johnny," continued C:map, "you see, Tammy, that question can seriously expose the reason why one's in the music industry as a Christian."

"Really? Care to explain to our audience?" asked Tammy.

"Sure, with pleasure," C:map sat up straighter. "Look at it this way: so many rappers mention god in their tracks, but Jesus said that we will know them by their fruit. So we know who is talking about Elohim and who is not. However, here's my question to those rappers who are Christian. Listen carefully now . . . if Jesus told us to deny ourselves, why would you want people to know that you a rapper, before they know that you a follower?"

"Interesting way to look at it," said Mrs. Banner, now interested.

"But you've given different ways of how you guys view the question, yet haven't actually answered it," said Tammy. "Let's do this, first and simple, what *exactly* are you trying to say?"

"Simple? We quick to say that Christianity is different to other religions, but not quick to want to be labeled differently in the music industry," said C:map.

"Yes, that's another great way to put it," agreed DJ Johnny, "we don't want to be labeled as another DJ/producer, or another hip hop artist. No, we want to be the salt of the industry. The city on a hilltop."

"I see. Back to the question then." Tammy shifted her focus onto the rapper, "C:map, are you a rapper that's Christian, or a Christian rapper?"

"With all that being said, I am a Christian rapper," said C:map, "my story is about how I was a rapper that was "Christian." I was a lukewarm Christian just abusing His grace. Not denying Jesus but not truly living for Him either. Then I heard, Yahshuandi, the Gospel Rapper, in the Rappers Behind Bars competition. I felt the words and I truly believe God spoke through him with that final rap. It wasn't long before I surrendered my life to the Lord and spent a year in His Word before I dared to spit in His name."

"I see, and you truly believe the industry needs this *now*?" asked Tammy, genuinely curious.

"No, the industry always had it. They just ignored it. It became a hidden genre only known to a few. Whether the industry needs it? No. I believe the *people* need it. They've had their ears watered

19

closed. It's about time that *truth* music opens them!" exclaimed C:map.

"Indeed it is!" DJ Johnny added with an exhilarated clap, "hear me when I say this: C. H. H. Ain't Dead . . ."

TWO

THE RAYS of the sun hit the city with full force, but the conditions mattered not when one entered North City Mall. The thick walls kept heat trapped inside whenever there was a lack of it outside. In this case, the air-conditioning kicked in to have the mall a place to run to as if seeking shelter.

Inside, a couple entered the CBM store, "Good afternoon. Yes, we are looking for the album of the artist that is currently touring his country?"

"Oh, wow . . ." Ruth Rennells was stunned, for that question rivaled the blue book query of earlier. "Normally artists tour their latest album," she said, "the best we can do is check new releases."

Ruth had the customers follow her past the books and into the music section of the store. It wasn't nearly as big as the reading content, but it served its purpose well.

"I see you guys have rock and rap albums," said the girlfriend, "I don't know if it will help, but it's a hip hop album we looking for."

"Yes," Ruth took a sharp turn. "That narrows the options, thank you, mam."

"For a youngster such as yourself, I would defs recommend some Aaron Cole," suggested another staff member, guiding a customer, in the section Ruth and the couple passed.

The boyfriend's eyes wondered without the knowledge of his girl.

"Do you remember any songs from the album?" asked Ruth.

"So Enjoyable . . ." slipped out of his mouth.

"Yes!" reacted the girlfriend, "sorry, I didn't mean to be loud. *So Enjoyable* was the song I heard on the radio. Thanks, babe."

"Hmm? Yeah, don't mention it," said the boyfriend, still halfway in his daze.

"Sorry, nothing's coming to mind," said Ruth, "but this here is our new hip hop releases," her hands were followed by their eyes. "Perhaps you'll recognize the name of the artist."

"Let's have a look," the girlfriend browsed at eye level, "I'm not noticing anything, babe, are you?"

Her boyfriend narrated as he browsed along with his fingertips, "Hmm, ASAP Preach, Bryann Trejo, I've heard of Bizzle through that Devil's Work response. I'm a Christian, know what I mean, so that song was really on point. Hmm, let's see . . . Dillon Chase –"

"Chase! Babe, I think it was him - where do you see that?" jolted the girlfriend in excitement, recognizing the surname. The boyfriend got the latest EP off the shelf, for Ruth was like a little girl who couldn't reach the cookie jar. It didn't bother her though. It was one cookie jar she had no intentions of reaching for anyway. She knew that the boyfriend would soon put the EP back.

It was obvious based on the way the girl reacted upon hearing the surname. She wasn't looking for *this* Chase's music. She was looking for another Chase's music. She was looking for *his* music. The Amborian born rapper clearly made a name for himself, locally and internationally. Good on him.

"Sooo, we found what we looking for?" Ruth asked, hoping she was wrong.

"Nooo," So Enjoyable wasn't listed. "It isn't *this* Chase," replied the girlfriend.

"Okay, if it isn't Dillon, could it be *Luke* Chase?" asked Ruth, fully aware of the coming response.

"Yes!" reacted the girlfriend, "sorry, about that. Yes, I think it's him."

"That guy on the radio?" the boyfriend got jealous at how she reacted to *just* the name, imagine if she saw him. "How sure are you that it's this *Luke* guy?"

"The name sounds more familiar –" replied the girlfriend.

"Can I ask you guys something?" Ruth stole their attention, "who do you guys normally listen to?"

"The big hip hop artists," said the boyfriend, "but this shop seems to be like a rip off of them, you know."

"A rip off? Why would you say that?" asked Ruth, slightly offended.

"Like we listen to J. Cole, but you guys have an artist called, *Aaron Cole*," replied the boyfriend.

"Oh, wow," Ruth fought hard not to laugh. The statement was nothing new to her. The secular artist would always be more known than those in its sub-genre form. Reason why it became the hidden, and not the underground, genre.

"No, it has nothing to do with ripping people off," the couple weren't regulars, and definitely wouldn't be back any time soon, so there would be no harm in setting them straight. "Like if I remember correctly, the mainstream has many artists with, *lil-something*, or *young-something* as a stage name. And I don't hear them claiming rip off rights."

"You say that as if it's an actual thing, but I get what you mean," said the boyfriend.

"These artists that we promote, some have made more albums than some of the big hip hop artists, sir. They just have a different message than the mainstream," concluded Ruth.

"So, it *is* Luke Chase, right?" asked the girlfriend as if Ruth had not stated anything of importance.

"Yes, it is," she gave up on them.

"And you guys don't stock his music?" asked the girlfriend.

"No, we do not . . ." replied Ruth, despondent.

"Have you even heard his new album? I really think you guys should consider stocking it."

"Mam –" started Ruth, but was quickly cut off by the girlfriend again, "If the album is as good as *So Enjoyable*," she said, "then you yourself should invest in a copy."

"Sure," replied Rennells, "I will consider it."

"It will be the best decision you make this year," the girlfriend concluded. Finally.

The boyfriend gave Ruth Rennells an apologetic look as the couple left the store. The CBM staff member nodded in acceptance. She understood. Fan girls had a way of being too much, even for their partners.

Isaac entered the store, gasping for air. His lungs were cooking like chops from the unexpected strain, "Turn – the radio on – please."

+++

A celebrity stood on the balcony absorbing the sun's gaze on him. Hotel staff were given permission to enter with the luggage left at the front counter. The celebrity ignored them. They had their jobs to do and he didn't need to thank them for doing what they got paid to do. Besides, his attention was on a more breathtaking image.

The Grand Fortuna Arena, a spaceship looking stadium, was inspiration itself. After the first attempt failed, a new construction company took over the project and they really hit the nail on the head.

The celebrity turned to take in the apartment he would be staying in. He couldn't believe it. Such luxury was only two hours from the city he was born in. If only he knew back then.

Nah, what would have been the point of such knowledge back then? It wouldn't have changed the fact that he couldn't afford an hour in this room.

From humble beginnings he came. Who would have thought he would be performing at one of Amboria's iconic stadiums tomorrow night? Like the stadium, he himself was an inspiration!

He more than anyone deserved to throw himself onto the five-star bed. It was as soft as a marshmallow and comforted the spine as if the creators used him as inspiration. The size of the plasma complimented his ego pretty well. So why not put it to use? The first channel the TV suggested was *North City Visuals.*

Let's see how they promoted the album back home.

He put the remote down and the TV rebelled. Instead of him being the only one promoted. It threatened with some DJ Johnny and C:map: they were about to perform their new track called, *Purpose For Living.*

"Haven't heard of you guys, but that's a dope title," he assumed the genre, "now, spit some bars!"

DJ Johnny began the instrumental as if he was waiting for Luke Chase's go ahead.

+++

Isaac greeted all in one go before he apologized to Ruth for being late.

"It's okay," she said as they got to the radio, "your mother phoned to let us know."

"Yes, she mentioned so," replied Isaac.

"What station are you looking for?"

"I don't know the number," he admitted, "I just know that it's the North City Radio Station."

"Oh, wow, that sure helps . . ." said Ruth, sarcastically.

"Ninety-one point two," said an old lady, who knew what station they were talking about, "it's the best in the city."

The staff members thanked the customer in unison. Ruth turned the sphere ball on the system until she got to the number given, so Isaac's excitement upon hearing the artist's voice was unnecessary.

"You're like a regular fan girl," mumbled Ruth. "Who's this guy anyway?"

There was no response. Isaac was already absorbed in the lyrics of the song. Even though he was late for the performance, which was nothing new, he caught the flow immediately.

(C:map)

So you found your purpose?
Your purpose for living is what you follow
All in His glory!
Live each day like there's no tomorrow

What would Jesus do?
A question one tries to ask

25

Narrow path only for a few
Broken, yet held together like a cast
Oh, that Jesus teaching too ancient?
What about the new commandment?
I swear He coming soon
But you ain't got time to be patient?
The world got you rushing for glory
Became a self proclaimed god like Nimrod
Told the whole world an inspiring story
Left out the surrender of your soul in the fog
The future looked nonexistent
The past seemed irrelevant
So you built a tower everyone looking up can see
Let their eyes leave Elohim without saying, "Worship Me . . ."

So you got the haters jealous?
But they don't know you feeling hollow
All about making money!
Live each day like there's no tomorrow

So you found your purpose?
Your purpose for living is what you follow
All in His glory!
Live each day like there's no tomorrow

+++

"What . . . nonsense is this?" Luke asked as if TVs in luxury rooms spoke back. "Where's the real bars? Not this . . . stuff."

The celebrity left the plasma in the condition he found it. The artist on screen was without a doubt Amborian, just like him. Had they met before? Nah, he would have surely remembered it.

Luke couldn't afford to be distracted the night before his final show. Was that it? Was that the plan of this artist? Nah, what would he gain from that? The celebrity was clearly overthinking and had to get these thoughts out of his head before they became poison. *Liquor.*

He picked up the phone next to the bed.

26

"Room service," said a voice on the other side. "How may I help you?"

Nah, he couldn't. Luke didn't drink the day before, nor the day of the show. He preferred to be focused. Plus, liquor blocked out any second thoughts that would usually cross his mind.

He tried liquid of a different kind though. Just stood there under the supplier and let it rain down on him. Still, the thoughts would not disappear. If anything, the shower made it worse.

Was this artist dissing him? *Liquor.* Nah, it's *just* an art. A song he wrote. The words weren't directly to him. It couldn't be.

+++

(C:map)

So you got the haters jealous?
But they don't know you feeling hollow
All about making money!
Live each day like there's no tomorrow

So you found your purpose?
Your purpose for living is what you follow
All in His glory!
Live each day like there's no tomorrow

What would Jesus do?
The answers are all in the Gospels
Part of a chosen few
Like when Jesus chose the disciples
This part is for none other
You can't give up, my brother
Last night, He was your visitor
It's been three days, my brother
Yes, the final is where you lost
Yes, the family mentor is lost
Break out of that depression - you are not alone
It's now time for resurrection - move that stone
For you know the purpose He has for your life

THE HIDDEN GENRE

Pray, rise and spread the Word of Christ
You have become stronger through this trial
But first! You need to go and reconcile

The hook zoned to the background.

What was happening? It started with last night's sudden urge to write. Then the accident. The officer. The narrow path. The radio for updates. The song . . .

Isaac's thoughts were written all over his face.

"Is something wrong?" asked Ruth to no avail. Unsurprisingly, although the song was over, her colleague was still absorbed in the lyrics as he left. This artist on the radio wrote about something very personal. Closer to home than he may know.

Ruth couldn't play dumb when she felt it too. That feeling when one knows exactly why something happened, but convince oneself that it couldn't be for *that* reason. That the song couldn't have been structured to directly confront the two artists she knew personally.

For as much as the competition was three years ago, sometimes, it felt like it was yesterday when Isaac Banner lost to Luke Chase.

THREE

THE CREW for the event put their all into preparations. The dark outfits they wore made the heat work as hard as them. Most of the men had their shirts drenched in sweat. Some of the women made sure to be within sight, as they "worked" with different movements than the guys. Either way, they prepared the stage for a once in a life time performance.

Regardless of their efforts, Luke stared over the sea of empty seats in amazement. Did the label really expect to fill this amount of seats? Yes, he had a one in a million agent on his side. Even better, he had fans worldwide on his side, but wasn't this asking too much?

"You here early," said agent Dobe as he took his stance next to the celebrity. "What? The hotel not good enough?"

"Nah, it ain't that," replied Luke, "I just needed to clear my head. That's all."

"Well, get this into your head," the agent guided his client's eyes around the stadium, "fifty thousand seats will be filled tomorrow night." A grin overtook the bottom of his face, "Didn't I say we would conquer the world?"

"You did and I'm truly grateful for everything you've done, Nick. I mean it . . ." said Luke.

"Hey, I don't get all the credit. You brought a lot to the table as well, don't forget that. Look at those seats . . . those are from your flows, not mine. And the songs are what the fans are enjoying. Not my little agent speeches."

"Yeah, but you got me the right gigs, the right interviews, at the right moments. That's why I am where I am today," said Luke, "I was nothing but a rapper caught in a struggle hidden from the world. You got me out of it. You basically saved my life, Nick. Thank you. It really means a lot to me."

Agent Dobe sneaked a look at his client. Now he was curious. Luke was acting way too . . . humble. Was it because he was at the end of his contract and in his feelings, or because he was so close to home after three years?

Nick lit a cigarette and wished he could blow his doubts away like he did the smoke, "I'm really honored to represent you, Chase. Your raw talent is what got me interested in signing you. That's no joke, kid. We would have done anything to get you and look how worth it, it has been."

"Yeah," Luke's eyes wondered around the arena, "it sure has been worth it, hasn't it?"

"Come on, kid - where's the energy? I can't have you perform like this tomorrow. You'll bore your fans to death," said a now concerned Nick.

Behind them, a member hesitated to approach. She looked towards the other crew members as if she needed confirmation that her job wasn't on the line for doing this.

"Hi, Mr. Chase. I'm a huge fan! So, I'm really excited for tomorrow night. That's why . . . well. We need to prepare the floor. So, can you please clear the stage?" asked the fan/crew member who tried to keep her composure.

"Sure -"

"But you can stay a little longer if you want to," she quickly added.

"Nah, I'm all good," grinned Luke.

+++

"You said you wanted to chat about something," Luke continued the conversation in the front row, "is it feedback on what I've requested?"

"Listen, Luke, you know I've had your back since the beginning, right," Nick stated more than questioned. "Decep Records are willing to offer you a three album contract over a period of seven years. I think you should accept it."

"What you mean, seven years?" Luke asked, curious. "How exactly would that work?"

"We still in detailed discussions," replied Nick, "but manage your money right and it will guarantee a paycheck every week for seven years."

"A paycheck every week for seven years," repeated Luke in disbelief, "I like the sound of that."

"But remember, it's all because of how successful this album has been. The one you will be performing tomorrow night. 'Luke! Chase! Conquer!' has broken records no one expected it to. This album is one of the greatest ever released . . ." Nick went on.

"I couldn't agree more," replied Luke and he could sense that it was as if the agent thought Luke Chase may slip up tomorrow. He hadn't done that once and they've been touring for two whole years. What would be the reason now?

"I understand the importance of *this* album, Nick. I don't think you need to worry about me," continued Luke, "but since you mentioned that they willing to offer me a new contract, that means you've been in contact with them. Does that also mean my request has been granted?"

Agent Dobe nodded with a grin, but it was half hearted. It was as if he wanted Luke to get rewarded for all the hard work, but not like this.

+++

Isaac was on his lunch break in the back room when Ruth walked in to check on the stock they were hiding from customers, "Hey, just thought you should know I'm heading to the studio later. Been working on a song since last night. Your mother said you were busy with a track as well." Ruth turned to Isaac, "So, I thought maybe we could go together or something."

Isaac, tilting slightly on the chair, nodded his head like he was overexcited to be alone with her. On closer inspection, he was listening to music, but not with headphones. He was using her AirPods while his equipment charged. She forgot about that.

Slightly embarrassed and annoyed, considering that this was the third time he hadn't spoken back, Ruth decided to scare him for revenge.

Isaac was glued into the company's Facebook account. He wasn't the type to start his own and the manager allowed him to use theirs, so why not? The news was reporting officers being attacked and firearms being swiped. This happened at the scene of the horrific accident that held up the traffic. Investigations were ongoing to whether the truck driver was involved.

Was Officer Den okay? Isaac sure hoped so.

Ruth sneaked up slowly. Like a tortoise. Every step mattered. Every step echoed nothing. With such tip toe walking, one would have thought her to be a regular high heels girl. Such silence only seen in horror movies. Even without earphones, Isaac wouldn't have heard her. Her breathing stopped. She was close enough to sink her lips on his neck. Close enough to unleash the tension they were building. Too close. She was too close.

"Hey, Ruth!" Isaac gave them both a fright.

"Oh, wow, why you shouting?" Ruth shouted back in shock.

"Why were you - never mind," Isaac passed the AirPod on the table to her, "check this out."

Did he actually hear what she said and ignored her on purpose?

Ruth would so give him an ear full right now, but the breaking news was more important than the mischievous grin on Isaac's face.

Breaking News:

Luke Chase to perform last show in North City.

"He's going to perform at home?" they questioned in unison.

THE HIDDEN GENRE

"Luke Chase will still be performing at the Grand Fortuna tomorrow night," said Tammy on North City News, "and then he will be having the final show the following weekend."

"Only the following weekend? But that's like a two hour drive from here. Why not have two shows in two nights?" asked Isaac, to no one in particular.

"It wouldn't surprise me if the girls go to the concert there and then here the following weekend," said Ruth, who never understood why the women drooled over celebs.

"I'm more surprised that he would have his last concert here on his birthday weekend," said Isaac. "Do you think Luke requested it?"

"Honestly? I don't know, Isaac. I would like to believe that he would like to use the opportunity to visit, but lately . . ." Ruth's head and voice dropped.

"No, I refuse to believe he would stoop so low, Ruth," Isaac used the method of energy his mom always used on him, "if it's about money, then it's probably the agent's idea."

"How can you be so sure?" asked Ruth of Isaac's optimism.

"It's just . . ." he shifted his eyes to another reporter who came into view as if interested in what he was saying, "I just have a feeling, Ruth. Think about it, the story of the three year contract ends where it started -"

"So it ends where it all began," said the reporter with a grin like he was listening to their conversation, "but the question everyone should be asking is this: which Luke Chase will end up performing that night?"

The reporter left that in the air for the city to ponder on. It was a good question that only the locals would understand. The two CBM staff members gazed at each other in amazement.

Will Luke Chase perform the independent album that got him into the Rappers Behind Bars competition (that he later won), or will he perform the new album that the world embraced?

They had a feeling it would be the latter. But they were in for a huge surprise.

Their eyes formed a bridge for their souls to connect. Ruth's features were gorgeous and urges that one wasn't suppose to have for a friend tried to take charge. But to Isaac, Ruth was more than a

33

friend though. He didn't know her thoughts on the topic, thus such a confession could cause the departure of their friendship . . . for ever. He risked it not and forced himself out of her soul to the screen's safe haven . . . for now.

Ruth kept at it. There was something different about her colleague. He was no longer upset about the loss, at least compared to the last three years he wasn't. But nor did he seem content about it. Then again, this was the first time they spoke about Luke in six months.

Oh, wow, was Isaac hiding something from her?

FOUR

IT WAS night shift for the sky but half the moon pitched up, the other half was kept in the dark.

Chantal pulled into the parking lot of the church building and gave the vehicle a rest; like the entire journey, her daughter's eyes were still ahead of her like she had a staring contest with a ghost. The building's lights snapped her back to reality.

"I guess Isaac's here already," said Chantal.

"Thanks for the lift," said Ruth, getting ready to exit the car.

"Whoa, slow down there, girly," she hated to see her daughter depressed, especially since they worked so hard to get her out of it. "You've practically been quiet since you got home. There's something bothering you and I know you only really speak with your dad, but I want you to know I'm here for you. If you need to talk about anything, even deeper level stuff, then don't hesitate to come to me."

"Oh, wow, was the small talk not convincing enough?" said her daughter, sarcastically.

"I'm your mother, girly. You can't fool me that easily," replied Chantal.

Her mother was right. Maybe it was time Ruth let her in. Maybe her mother stopped comparing her to her older sister. Maybe she actually wanted to get to know her second daughter. "Okay," Ruth closed the door. "First, you do know that Luke is coming, right -"

"I want you to stay far away from that, kid!" Chantal began lecturing, "he's the reason why -"

"Mother stop!" Ruth cut her off.

Clearly nothing had changed.

"I'm sorry, Ruth," replied her mother.

Clearly nothing . . . had she *just* used her name? No, it couldn't be. Chantal didn't. It was her imagination, it had to be. Ruth hadn't heard her name leave the lips of her mother for nearly three years now.

"I can't help it that I get emotional pretty quick." Chantal snapped the seat belt out, "okay . . ." she turned to face her daughter, "I will try to sit here, keep quiet and listen to you speak."

"I don't want you to *just* listen, mommy," Chantal's heart sank upon hearing the word *mommy* from her daughter's mouth. It was so sweet to her ears. *Mother* had become such a bitter word that Ruth only used as a counter to everything. "I want to hear *your* thoughts about it. How you feel about situations, what you did when you were in similar positions. Like you did with Casey - but I need you to let me finish first."

Chantal surrendered into her seat after an agreement was made, "This isn't about Luke," said Ruth before she zoned out as if the ghost returned for round two, "it's about Isaac . . ."

"What about Isaac?" her mother finally asked, after she was a hundred percent sure it was her time to speak.

"I think he knows," whispered Ruth.

Chantal swallowed the bile in her throat, "Knows what?"

"About Luke -"

"I didn't mean to keep -" said Chantal, until her daughter cut her off by adding, "and me . . ."

"Oh . . ." Chantal's breathing rhythm slowly returned, "I don't think it's that then."

Ruth's forehead wrinkled. "How can you be so sure?"

"I just have a feeling . . ."

THE HIDDEN GENRE

Same question Ruth asked Isaac. Same answer given. Was it really a feeling they had, like the feeling her and Isaac had about Luke's final performance, or were they actually hiding something from her?

"Plus, knowing Isaac," Chantal quickly added, "I think he would have said something if he knew."

"I don't know about that mother," said Ruth.

So, it was back to *mother* again?

"Isaac can be very shy at times," she continued, "it's the whole reason why I think he gives me mixed signals." Her eyes found the gear box, "I don't think I'll be getting married anytime soon."

"Is *that* what this is all really about?" asked Chantal. Ruth's silence was an answer enough. "Let me clarify this," Chantal sat up straighter. "Just because I found your father when I was 19, doesn't mean you must do the same. Yes, you are turning 19 in a few months time. Yes, Isaac will be a great husband to have. But the decision isn't *just* in your hands," she grabbed her daughter's full attention with that final statement, "you need to understand that he has a goal in life –"

"And just because I dropped out of school, that means I don't have any goals in life?" snapped Ruth.

Chantal gave her daughter a *like really* glance. Even though Ruth contradicted herself, Mrs. Rennells was slightly proud to see a bit of herself in her second daughter too. Sometimes speaking without listening had its benefits. Other times it didn't.

"Isaac wants to preach through music with a secular record label for a living," continued Chantal, "not one label has gotten back to him, which honestly, I don't think he's surprised. The competition three years ago was meant to be his break through, they promised a three year deal to the winner, regardless of the artist's content. But he lost in the finals. Then a few days later, he lost his father in that horrific accident. That is a lot to deal with, Ruth."

It wasn't Ruth's imagination after all, "But it has been three years now, mommy. Three *whole* years."

"Three *difficult* years," corrected Chantal, "imagine your dream got shattered, and then you lost your father as well, all in the space of three days. Then while you are dealing with all that, your best friend is too busy living his dream to even care."

"Oh, wow . . ."

A part of Ruth wanted to ask her mother how she knew so much about him, but the other, the part that wanted to see Isaac and hold him for comfort like she should have back then, that side won.

+++

Within the walls, most people would have thought the door of the store room was open. But not Ruth. To her, the door of the studio was open.

The current instrumental flooded the place with bass, or noise, dependent on age. There was no one in the seats to witness the flames coming from the speakers. Then the track stopped as if upset that its talent was being slept on by the masses. The speakers gave off sharp dinosaur screeches before the familiar beat took control again. Ready for round two.

Now
It's time to go reconcile

(Yahshuandi, the Gospel Rapper)

Lord, You know me first hand
You know the hairs on this head
Lord, I am nothing but a young man
And fame probably would have gotten to my head
Or maybe it's just another Saul - Paul situation
So he be in that pre-Damascus occupation?
Guide me when I finally speak up
Hide me in plain sight when enemies sneak up

The instrumental was given a solo piece like a guitarist. However, it didn't last long. Ruth slowly sat down and the volume mimicked her.

"One - two. Testing, one - two."

She heard Isaac's voice.

Man, have I really gone three years without it?
Lord, show me how to go about it and not make her doubt it

THE HIDDEN GENRE

See, I ain't worried about her bun size
Those rappers are as common as the sunrise

Ruth's heart jumped into her throat . . .

But I can feel it, I know she feel it, we just got that heat
Ultimate goal: to worship together, not her being naked

Rennells' blood rushed to her head . . .

Appearance don't matter when her inner beauty is what I seek
Oh, wow, I just got distracted

Ruth Rennells would later find herself on the floor.
Wait, had he just used her *oh wow* words?
Isaac hastily got up to check if Ruth was there, "And she says *I'm* always late."
A part of him was relieved she hadn't come yet. The biggest part of him was happy she hadn't heard all that.
Isaac took a couple more seconds just in case. The bathroom lights down the hall were still off. She wasn't there. She probably wasn't in the building yet. Why was he so worried anyway? It's not like it would be a bad thing for her to find out. Wasn't he, being early, already too much of a sign to begin with?
Isaac wished he could lock his feelings away like he did the studio door. They both shared the same properties to begin with. It was always open and could only be locked from the inside. He restarted the track and went for another go at the mic.

(Ruth Rennells)

Father God You sent Your Son
For us
Jesus Christ You walked among
Us

Holy Spirit guide my ways
Jesus Christ! He only saves

THE HIDDEN GENRE

Forgive as you have been forgiven
Now
It's time to go reconcile

(Yahshuandi, the Gospel Rapper)

Father, You are strong when I am weak
Son, You said to turn the other cheek
Holy Spirit, please guide what I speak
Cause the world goes with the opposite of meek
I can't live for You
And rely on something like flesh feelings
I can't live for You
And rely on human beings
You said that man will fail me every time
I can't match You even in my prime
Broken . . . When I lost my earthly father
Chosen . . . Then to represent my heavenly Father
I trust the signs that You have shown
I trust that You believe I'm grown
It's time I step out and approach him
It's time I get loud and coach them
It's time for the world to re-acknowledge You
It's time for the world to re-acknowledge You

(Ruth Rennells)

Father God You sent Your Son
For us
Jesus Christ You walked among
Us

Holy Spirit guide my ways
Jesus Christ! He only saves
Forgive as you have been forgiven
Now
It's time to go reconcile

The instrumental saw itself out. Isaac would wait for his partner in music to arrive before he signed and sealed his part of the song. He sat down, pulled out his phone to message Ruth, when a different instrumental took the old one's place.

Ruth's eyes snapped open. She heard a voice. Why and how was she on the floor? Never mind that. That wasn't important right now. The sound she heard was deadly familiar. It wasn't Isaac or a stranger's voice. It was *hers*.

Lord, I've been reading that prison letters
I've been trying to rid these burden pressures

No. Worse. It was her rapping. She needed to stop it. Singing was how everyone knew her. Only one person knew she rapped and she preferred it that way. The raps were way too personal.

My family has done well while I lag behind
Lord, help me understand that You are beyond time

Oh, wow! Of course the studio door was locked from the inside. Only one option left.

See, my sister became a famous detective
My mother got married around the same age
I wonder if I am to follow those steps
Or should I keep my feelings caged?

She entered the electrical room.

Lord, when I lost her, I felt like my life was done
Now I like this dude with the same name as Abraham's –

The power went off . . .

THE HIDDEN GENRE

FRIDAY NIGHT

FIVE

THE ONLY heat on offer was from the heater and the bars the artist was spitting. Margarette Kane pulled to the side of the road and picked up, hopefully, the last fan. She hopped into the back seat with an ear to ear smile.

Who wouldn't be excited? They were on their way to the much anticipated concert. North City Radio had spent the past hour promoting it. The blonde girl in the passenger seat cranked up the volume upon hearing the *Ladies Love Luke* track.

Margarette checked her mirror as she heard a window open, but her brunette friend gave her a *lighten up* look after she tossed an overworked joint out. The robots flicked orange and then red in one smooth movement, forcing her to bring the car to a halt. The back row seats had twice the amount of girls than the front, one would have thought that Luke Chase was making the music video back there.

The robot granted them permission to continue their journey towards the island. They were nearly by the bridge that made no attempts to grab Fortuna Island, unlike women when they saw Luke Chase.

+++

The girls got onto one of the many ferries with screaming fans, who probably would've been quiet if there weren't any cameras. Many clearly left not just their cars, but their dignity behind as well.

Margarette was here to do more than celebrate her old friend. She was proud of his success. He brought himself out of the depths of poverty. Sadly, the people inside didn't even know that Luke once walked among them. The very thought had become nothing but a rumor that lurked itself into extinction.

The ferry pulled up to the port on the huge island. The Grand Fortuna Arena stood there in the center like it demanded attention.

The height challenged the skyscrapers. The width made them look skinny. One would have assumed the humans were boarding a space ship ready to leave earth.

+++

Inside the arena, fans took their seats and absorbed the atmosphere. The girls, that Margarette picked up along the way, had decided to form a fan club with her and her brunette best friend.

"Gabi, please keep my seat for me," said Margarette.

"Hey, Kane, remember we came to have fun," said the brunette as she grabbed Margarette's hand, "not to score."

"But didn't you say *you* wanted to score with Chase?"

It was the main reason why Margarette kept secret the past friendship she had with the celebrity. If her best friend knew, she would never hear the end of it.

"Yeah, stop changing it to me," said Gabi with a guilty smile, "you know exactly what I'm talking about."

"I just need to confirm something," Margarette broke away from the group of girls. "I'll be back before the concert starts, don't worry."

"Why would I be worried about having Luke all to myself?"

+++

An eruption of cheers could be heard outside the arena. A reporter, not from NCN, watched as a limo pulled up at the entry point. Silence overcame the crowd as a man got out of the driver seat and walked to what was assumed to be the celebrity's side.

"Everyone's awestruck here at the arrival of Luke Chase," said the reporter, "one would think he was a king from a distant land coming to claim his spaceship. Get it? Because –"

"Whack reporters like you are the reason why people watch North City News instead of any other news outlets!" commented one of the fans, who was verbally ignored, but the disgust on the reporter's face wasn't hidden from those watching on their televisions.

The doors to the limo opened and the cheers completely gave him a reason to continue his job. He was to report the show, but the fans had no mercy for those at home trying hear what was said. He tried raising his voice as Luke Chase stepped out to greet his supporters.

The celebrity stood there, either amazed at his support, or was it him giving the fans more time to praise him? The answer hung on the opinion one had of him.

There were a few men in the crowd and it reminded Luke of his critics: how they were a few needles inside a massive haystack of supporters.

A smile accidentally broke out, which got the girls even more excited. Some fans needed to fan themselves down. His facial features were enough to have any girl make a sexual remark, if not lust for his touch.

Security came out of the limo and took their positions around the celebrity. Luke Chase was given the go ahead.

"As you can see, if you are able to ignore all the flashes, Luke Chase is sure to take pictures and sign autographs with his supporters," the reporter continued to report arguably every detail. "And now he has entered the building. Ladies and gentlemen, Luke Chase has entered the building . . ."

+++

The crowd began to settle down as they drew nearer to the start of the show. Luke watched from backstage as he looked upon his fans like he was trying to spot someone he knew.

No one . . .

A few fathers and mothers with their daughters, that were around sixteen, prepared themselves for the show of a lifetime. Some lyrics were not appropriate for such an age, even if you put a filter on it. Luckily, most of the fans were young women, and that was the audience he was going for. But regardless of what anyone said, he really tried to make the album for both genders. So the lack of men was slightly disappointing. Then again, he remembered how he enjoyed the boy bands, but you would never have seen him at a concert, regardless of whether he had the money or not, he had to be seen as "hard," and boy bands were for girls.

"Mr. Chase?" the event manager finally found the celebrity, "I don't know why you are so confident, but because you requested no opening acts. You on in fifteen."

"Yeah, I know . . ." said Luke.

The event manager gave him a thorough look and with a friendly smile said, "No, I don't think you know. I don't think you ready either . . . can I get a make-up artist for Mr. Chase please?"

Luke wasn't going to let an event manager control the way he mentally prepared himself for a show. The celebrity escaped the moment the manager began his search for a make-up artist.

+++

"Hey stop!" yelled a security guard, "you're not allowed to be back here!"

Kane ran like a thief being chased. She had a slim body and gained momentum with every turn. The security guard's only hope was calling back-up and just in time, back up came. The security ran flat into another member of the team. Margarette ran straight into Luke, who had been running like he himself had cold feet. However, he was the exact person she was searching for.

"I'm sorry . . . here, let me help you," Luke offered her a hand up after they gathered her things. "What's with the CDs? Normally people have me sign mine, not theirs."

"I'm not here for an autograph," Margarette didn't take the offer for she feared that it would have given him a hold over her. She was so worried about being handed over to the men in black, that she hadn't noticed her necklace escaped from under her shirt.

"Is that right?" Luke waved his security away and left his other hand there in the air, "then tell me exactly what you're here for, Miss . . ."

"Kane. Margarette Kane," she shook his outstretched hand after being sure the security was gone, "I'm here to *score* a record deal."

"A record deal? And you think an artist can give out a contract like that?" asked a curious and sarcastic Luke.

"No, but I know that *you* know people who do."

"Yeah, fair enough. Let's see what you got then . . ."

"Just like that?" asked a surprised Kane.

Luke used his head and neck muscles to answer the question.

"You not going to listen to my music? You want me to rap right now, without a speaker?" it was too easy, "you know it will sound much better with a speaker -"

"I got a concert to get to, . . ." it sounded like her name was already forgotten.

Margarette ignored it, cleared her throat, and prepared herself.

(Mkay)

Left the state with the future in my hands
Nothing but successfulness in my plans
No worries when I'm able to keep my stomach full
Now I'm coming back empty like the prodigal
So much money just covering that emptiness
Started throwing questions and found Jesus

"Stop -"

You'd

"Stop -"

Probably

"Stop right there!" exclaimed Luke, getting her to stop, "it's just as I thought."

"I know," Margarette tested him, "that's why I told you it will sound much better with a speaker."

"Nah, it ain't that," he gave her necklace one more glance as if he needed to confirm that it was a cross, "you actually got skill, but I suggest you walk away now before it's too late." Luke walked right past her as if he volunteered to show her how, "This industry just ain't for a rapper like you."

SIX

TONIGHT WOULD be the first night Luke had a drink before a show. He went to the *after party* room with a one track mind, for only alcohol could help him rid the thoughts:

Why did these Christian rappers keep showing up? Was he their target for some unknown reason? And if so, why him? There's so many secular artists, why weren't they annoying them? *Liquor.*

He opened another door within the room that led to liquor paradise. Only then Luke noticed that he had a gun to his head. His heart jumped into his throat. He was okay with guns, but not okay with the gore they left people in from this distance. He gave the person a quick check in the mirror, but the human had his face covered with a mask.

"Look, man, I'm seriously not in the mood for this," he put a drink down and slowly faced the intruder. "Take whatever you want and get going."

"I don't know where you grew up, boy," came a deep laugh as the person closed the door, but was careful not to lock it, "but where I'm from, which is in the heart of North City, the man with the gun calls the shots." The masked man kept his focus on Luke as he walked backwards to go lock the first door, "I just want to have a *special* drink with you."

"Whatever you getting paid, I can pay double," Luke started to panic, "I'm a famous celebrity that helps homeless children, you don't want to kill me, man. Think about the –"

"Shut up and sit down!" shouted the masked gunman.

Luke obeyed.

"We can talk about *that* paycheck later," the man licked his lips as he glanced over the variety that the open bar offered. "I really couldn't believe all the expensive drinks you have at a snap of your fingers. You over-privileged, boy . . . by the way," the man took a sip of a bottle that was kept aside, "I'm not here to kill you –"

"You just damn well said you want me to drink poison!" said Luke, with a hint of rage in his voice.

"Your language, boy," he pointed the weapon and Luke went mute. "Who would have thought? You don't just talk crap in your music, apparently you do so in real life as well." The man pulled out two tubes of water-like substances and put one back, "I said that I want you to drink something *special*. I never said poison." He poured it into a cup and mixed it with alcohol like a bartender, "I just don't want you to perform for a little while, that's all."

"Not perform? I don't get it? What will you gain from that?" asked Luke.

"Simple: a paycheck that's worth more than the tips I earn in a year." He signaled for the celebrity to get up, "This will have you lose your *pretty* voice for a couple weeks. Now drink it!"

Luke had to obey or risk being shot. He came here to the room to have a drink and get thoughts out of his head. The latter surely worked, but he wasn't so sure he wanted a drink anymore. The celebrity slowly reached for the cup offered to him.

What was taking security so long? This guy locked the entry door, didn't he? That should have triggered the panic button. The door should have been kicked in by now.

"I don't get it . . ." said Luke, trying to stall for time.

"*What* don't you get, boy?" asked the gunman.

"I don't understand why you need a gun when you so adamant on not killing me," Luke looked at the foam cup in his hand. "You should have just kidnapped me, how can I be sure this drink won't take me out for good?" asked Luke, curious of the intentions now.

"You'd be dead by now if I wanted to kill you, that's how," replied the gunman, weapon still point blank at Luke's forehead.

"Fair enough . . ."

"I don't know why you even here to begin with," he added.

"What's that suppose to mean?" Luke's curiosity peaked.

"Stop asking questions and drink up already! I don't have all night, boy!" shouted the man with the weapon, clearly getting agitated at all the questions and clear stalling.

The door was hit hard from outside.

"Crap!" the consequences of being caught flashed before gunman's eyes. "Drink the damn *liquor*!"

Luke threw the liquid into the intruder's eyes and then delivered him into a new reality with a right hook. The trigger got pulled, but there was no gun shot. Did it jam, or did Luke mistake the sound for the guy's broken jaw?

The banging stopped and a voice was heard instead. It asked for the door to be shot down immediately.

"Don't shoot! I'm all good! Give me a second!" curiosity about the substance got the best of the celebrity. "I'm coming to open! Put the guns away . . ."

He let security in and they followed protocols.

+++

"I told you to have security everywhere you go, Mr. Chase, but no, you don't want to listen to me," the event manager was stressed, he went to grab a drink and swallowed it in one go. He pointed to the make-up artist, "We are already running late because of this. Please make sure Mr. Chase is –"

His voice died out.

"Yeah," said the celebrity, "that worked a little too fast for my liking."

"What worked too fast?" asked Nick as he entered. "Are you good, Luke?"

"I'm all good. This guy tried to mute me –"

"Mute you?" the agent looked upon the now unmasked man with rage, "like tried to *kill* you?"

"No, he must've had some other agenda," a man in casual clothes approached them, "the gun's fake."

So it wasn't that the masked man wouldn't kill him, he couldn't. Nah, he never wanted to. He got paid to make Luke silent for a while. Who was behind it? It couldn't have been the Christian artists. This was too extreme for them. Was the masked man working for those "music influences" people? They were more annoying than the recent come up of Christian rappers. Music was nothing but an art. You either got the skill or not. How on earth did it influence people?

"Who are you guys?" asked Nick.

"We are the NCPA, sir," replied the head of the team.

"North City cops? What are North City cops doing this side?" was the follow up question.

"We pretty much here to support our local rap star." The man turned to Luke, "Did this guy say anything of importance, son?"

"Wait, Luke don't answer that," interfered the agent. "*Who* exactly are you?"

"I already told you who I am," replied the cop.

"No, you told me who *they* are. The officers in uniform, they are North City cops. Not you. I've been living in this country long enough to know that the NCPA don't work in casual clothes. So who are you?" asked Nick, clearly still frustrated by the situation.

"Let me ask you this, do you really think I would be allowed to be at the scene if I wasn't a cop?".

Nick Dobe took a moment to consider the question. "I would still like to see a badge before you interview my client," he said, stubbornly.

"The ambulance has arrived, Captain," said an officer to the man in casual clothes. "Should we let them in?"

"That's pretty much their job," he replied, "let them do it." The Captain looked at Nick, "Will *you* allow me to do mine?"

Nick turned to watch the medical team patch up the intruder instead of answering.

"Son," the Captain faced the celebrity, "what did the man say before you messed up his pretty face?"

"Nothing much," said Luke, "I think he got paid to make sure I didn't perform tonight."

"These critics are going too far with this stunt -" said Nick, throwing in his side comments.

"Slow down there, Nick," the agent was hushed. The Captain focused on Luke again, "How was he to stop you from performing with a fake gun?"

"First, I don't think the critics were behind this, Nick. And sir, I'm curious, how do know it's a fake gun?" asked Luke.

"I understand your curiosity, son. But my question needs an answer first," replied the Captain.

"Fair enough," said Luke, "the guy, in a way, said that he got paid to prevent me from performing for a few weeks." Luke pointed to the table, "He put something in the drinks to do that."

Nick Dobe was beyond upset.

"So that's what the empty tubes are about? Pretty interesting case we have here." He pulled out the fake gun for the celebrity, "A deal is a deal. If you look closely, you can see the point has been taken off, that's where the orange plastic part use to be."

"No way . . ." gasped Luke in surprise that he didn't notice that in all his panic.

"Also," the Captain continued, "the handle as well as the trigger is different to ours. That's how we know what is fake and what isn't." The weapon, which was bagged, was given to Luke for examination, "As you can feel, it's pretty light too." He received the bag back, "It's great to hear that you treat every gun as a real threat. Let me tell you this, in the heat of the moment, it's very hard to tell the difference. If I could, I would give you a medal for the way you handled the situation."

"Thank you, sir," replied Luke, proud of himself.

"Most of all, I'm just glad you didn't try anything clever. My daughter is a huge fan and I don't know how I would've explained your death to her," he said, as if death was another word to him. "Anything else I need to know, son, or can we start clearing the drinks?"

The event manager gave up trying to explain to the make-up artist what he wanted done. He instructed Mr. Chase that it was time, or maybe he tried to say that the celebrity was beyond late. It was hard to tell.

"Nah, I'm all good." Luke Chase grabbed an unopened bottle from the new crate as he left, "Thank you for your service, Captain."

SEVEN

THE CELEBRITY was led and trailed by security. Never had it been done before. Never had he been held at gun point before a show. Never had he drank the day of, never mind minutes before a performance. Guess there really was a first time for everything.

"Luke! Chase! Conquer!" he heard, "we've witnessed nothing greater!"

The noise echoed throughout the stadium and got louder as he got closer to the end of his contract.

"I don't think he can hear us," DJ Smacks stopped the beat.

Luke had one more show after this; straight in the heart of North City. He would finally get to see his friends. Visit his home. Encounter more Christian rappers. *Liquor.* Was it really . . . worth it? *Liquor.* Was he . . . willing to endure it? *Liquor.* He continued to gulp at the bottle in his hand.

"Let's try calling for him again!"

Thoughts became unknown to Luke's brain. The very meaning of the word was lost on him. All that it processed was here and now as the event crew came to his aid.

The DJ continued to rile up the crowd, "Louder this time!" he yelled. "Luke! Chase! Conquer! We've witnessed nothing greater!" He turned up the instrumental adding fuel to the fired up crowd.

"Luke! Chase! Conquer!" they yelled back, "we've witnessed nothing greater!"

The celebrity stood on a platform under the stage getting final checks like a car before being given the stamp of approval; this included the nearly empty bottle of alcohol being taken away.

"Here we go, Mr. Chase," a staff member gave him a mic instead.

"He's ready to go," said another.

"Let's do this!" Luke Chase pumped himself up to conquer.

The platform lifted him to the top with pace as if it tried to mimic how he rose in the industry. Luke popped out of the ground in an all white outfit with henchmen covering the entire stage. The lights around the stadium got shy at the very sight of the celebrity. In the darkness he stood firmly on the stage with neon lights radiating off his body as screams echoed throughout the Grand Fortuna.

Fifty thousand fans awaited a performance of a lifetime and unlike yesterday, where a sea of empty seats stared at him, tonight a sea of flash lights adored him. Luke Chase absorbed the atmosphere and went down to one knee. He smiled at the women trying to reach for him. The urge to jump into the crowd and travel on the lake of palms almost overcame him. He swayed slightly as he tried to maintain the pose. Focus. He needed to focus. He needed to let the music take over now more than ever. The cheers eventually died down in anticipation.

"Luke. Chase. Conquer.," he whispered into the mic, "you've witnessed nothing greater."

"Luke. Chase. Conquer.," copied the hypnotized dancers, "we've witnessed nothing greater."

The crowd got involved and the lights slowly found the courage to reveal the henchmen one by one. DJ Smacks cranked the beat to full bass as the lights came alive.

(Luke Chase)

Luke! Chase! Conquer!
You've witnessed nothing greater

THE HIDDEN GENRE

Done all this on my own
You can compare me to the Creator

Luke! Chase! Conquer!
You ain't got anybody greater
On top I stand alone
Don't compare me to the Creator

These rappers be like, "He'll need features to go Platinum."
But I left them dead to the world like Latin
These attention seekers be like, "You know I use to know Luke."
But you lost in my past like a finished book.
These haters be like, "All he does is boast."
But this is my work! I don't hang with ghosts
These fakers be like, "He's cool! Can't wait for him to choke
though."
But this is my work! And you the one that's broke bro
These enemies be like, "Give me a bullet, dawg."
But all they do is bluff themselves up like a frog
These celebrities be like, "His fifteen seconds will soon dim."
But your chances of being right are terribly slim
These agents be like, "Chase, I can make your music sound
better."
But my music earns me more than all their clients put together.
These fans be like, "I'd love Luke even if it were taboo."
But all I got for that is . . . 'I love you, guys, too!"

"Luke! Chase! Conquer!" the dancers finished in unison, "we've witnessed nothing greater!"

+++

The fans were getting their money's worth. Luke Chase performed most of the album and many of their favourite songs got the attention they were seeking from the celebrity himself. This included: *Ladies Love Luke, Money Goals, My Party Joint* and many more.

Security was on tight alert and the artist was informed during numerous breaks that jumping into the crowd would be skipped tonight. Another first in two years.

The concert was coming to an end. In a blink of an eye the fans had enjoyed themselves and came to the realization that it would all be over in the next five minutes or so. The feeling was unavoidable, but not unwelcomed either.

Luke Chase kept the known fan favourite, the song on their lips, for last. They were craving for *So Enjoyable* whole night. They would get their wish. The song was to be performed next and the half naked dancers were the only hint needed.

(Luke Chase)

I see her twerking
Oh, my attention she stole
The way that she be moving
Ain't on a stripper pole

Oh, she be on this body
Showing she can dance
My hands be on her booty
She already unzipped my pants?

I got her missing me
It's so enjoyable
Homie, I am free
It's so enjoyable
I got her craving D...
It's so enjoyable
She's thick up and down
And it's edible

She got the face
She got the lips
She got the hips
I'm calling dips
We ain't lovers but she be getting loud

She be outrageous when we be getting wild
Women keep saying that I am overrated
But they keep coming back cause I ain't outdated
Outside she's normal
Outside she's lazy
Outside she's formal
In bed she's crazy
Told you no feelings but you lost focus
Emotional? Got no time to notice
Crying but marriage was what she suggested
And haters . . . I'm the reason your girls are tried and tested

I got her missing me
It's so enjoyable
Homie, I am free
It's so enjoyable
I got her craving D...
It's so enjoyable
She's thick up and down
And it's edible

I see her twerking
Oh, my attention she stole
The way that she be moving
Ain't on a stripper pole

Oh, she be on this body
Showing she can dance
My hands be on her booty
She already unzipped my pants?

My focus . . .
Be all upon those curves
My touch . . .
Be affecting all those nerves
They want to know why I use so much bass?
And like, why would he really choose her?
And I be like, hmm, check your girl's face

I swear every night you playing fear factor
Got no time for levels
When we grinding - grinding
Got no time for devils
When I'm shining – shining
Told you I'm going gold, no more polished silver
But you got left out the game like a cropped picture
Young, with a number one before I hit my peak
My words ain't the only penetration that's deep

I got her missing me
It's so enjoyable
Homie, I am free
It's so enjoyable
I got her craving D . . .
It's so enjoyable
She's thick up and down
And it's edible

"Let me hear the ladies!" yelled DJ Smacks.

"I got him missing me
It's so enjoyable
Girl, I am free
It's so enjoyable
I got him craving these . . .
It's so enjoyable
He's thick up and down
And it's edible"

"Now let me hear the men!" yelled DJ Smacks.

I got her missing me
It's so enjoyable
Homie, I am free
It's so enjoyable
I got her craving D . . .
It's so enjoyable

THE HIDDEN GENRE

She's thick up and down
And it's edible

The men were so few that it sounded like a wave of depression hit the stadium. Luke Chase and the women ended up helping them after the arena was drowned in laughter. Daughters and mothers were laughing at their fathers' miserable attempts at singing.

"Thank you everyone! None of this would be possible without you. You are the life blood of my career. You guys are what keep me going. Some of you I'll see in North City, some I may only see again next year, but let me say this: My album is dedicated to all you guys! Dedicated to the mothers and fathers who took the time to bring their daughters to the shows. Keep that up parents. Your kids will return that love when you older. Who knows? When it's their turn to look after you, they may just return the favor and bring you to a Luke Chase concert in the year twenty forty-three!" Luke bowed with a smile in appreciation to the earthquake of cheers that erupted throughout the arena. "These fans be like –"

"I'd love Luke even if it were taboo!" screamed the crowd.

"But all I got for that is . . . 'I love you, guys, too!'"

+++

The concert was done, but Luke's night was far from it . . .

"Mr. Chase, you have a guest," informed a bodyguard.

"If it isn't a super model," he walked into a new assigned after party room, "then I'm busy –"

There the guest stood. His rival. The man he hadn't seen in three years. There across him . . . Isaac Banner stood.

EIGHT

THE PERFORMANCE left fans thirsty for more. They longed for the celebrity's return long after he had left the stage. The next destination was the one and only, North City, and some fans had already snatched themselves some tickets. They couldn't understand the reason behind it being a whole weekend later, but it didn't matter, the fans knew it would be worth the wait. Any Luke Chase concert was worth the wait.

Margarette had watched the celebrity closely as he left the stage with tight security. Her encounter with him was not expected from their side, but weren't they over doing it now? Was Luke that adamant of not running into another Christian rapper, or did her little stunt cause more damage than she thought?

She hoped everything was physically okay with her old friend, because spiritually it wasn't. "This industry just ain't for a rapper like you," his words still echoed in Margarette's mind.

"How far you have drifted, Lukey," she whispered to herself.

"Hey, Kane," Gabi moved slightly in the passenger seat. "Did you say something?"

"No, it's nothing," came the reply, "I was just thinking out loud."

"Oh," the brunette had a mischievous grin, "I thought I heard you say you *scored* for a moment."

"No," Margarette couldn't resist a smile at her best friend's emphasis, "the exact opposite actually."

"So you did say something after all?" Gabi asked, curious.

"Yes, I did, but I'll tell you tomorrow. *You*, who screamed her lungs out whole night, needs to sleep."

Margarette didn't know whether she would follow through with it. It wasn't as if the secret was toxic, or something that could hurt her best friend. It was more of the fact that it wasn't special anymore. Luke hadn't even recognized her earlier. She knew the trauma he had was bad, but this was something else. Plus, what Gabi didn't know couldn't overexcite her.

"You've been driving for a while now, Kane," Gabi closed her eyes. Fatigue had hit her in the face the moment they dropped off the final fan girl, "I may be resting my eyes, but don't hesitate to let me know when you need me to take over. Okay?"

"Okay . . ."

+++

"Long time no see," Isaac got strangely comfortable on the couch, "and just as long time no speak . . ."

Did he come all this way to be cheeky? Nah, he's not the type. He was here for one reason and one reason only. Luke would have to be patient to find out if he was right.

"Yeah, I've been busy, you know," the celebrity went to pour himself a drink and almost hesitated in asking the question, "would you like something?"

"No, I'm good for now," declined Isaac.

"You seem pretty comfortable," he sat and gulped it down with one go. "So . . ." this was going to be a long night. "Did you enjoy the performance?"

Isaac was beyond late for the concert. It was pure luck that he made it in time to catch the final track. "Do you *really* want me to answer whether I enjoyed your secular performance or not?"

"Look, man, you came here –" but he got cut off.

"I'm proud of you, Luke," Isaac sat up, "well, *proud* in a way."

How was the celebrity expected to respond to that? Isaac wasn't his father . . . but he was his best friend. *Former* best friend. Saying those words didn't automatically make the last three years disappear.

"You went from the orphanage to travelling the world in the space of only three years," Isaac added.

Luke loved being admired by people for his achievements. But it coming from Isaac just felt . . . weird; like he was bound to say something stupid anytime soon.

"Well, not the *whole* world, but you get what I mean," Isaac sat back again, "the way you put on a show for your fans, it's really entertaining. I can see now why the agent would have done anything to sign you."

"What's that suppose to mean?" asked a slightly insulted Luke.

"Like . . . I don't think I could have impacted the industry the way you have," he finally said. "I'm proud to see you living your dream, I may not be proud about the content you releasing -"

"Yeah, I was waiting for that," Luke got up to pour another. He was right, "I thought I could handle it, but hearing you say it to my face just makes me wonder if you still jealous, Isaac."

"I'm not jealous, bro," he stood up to stand by his words, "I just believe you can use your gift differently -"

"Let me guess, to spread the Word, right?" Luke swallowed the drink and it burned like the way he asked the question. "Just so you know, I'm planning on signing a new seven year contract with the label."

"Seven years? Seven years, Luke!" Isaac had to compose himself for he was slowly forgetting the reason he came. "Bro. Congrats on the achievement, but I didn't come to argue -"

"You don't mean that," Luke filled his cup again, "if you really were proud, or truly wanted to congratulate me -" he looked Isaac dead in the eyes, "you would agree to feature in a future album."

"Now you see," Isaac walked away to sit, "that's the part where I didn't come to argue."

"Just think about it for a second," in the blink of an eye Luke was opposite his rival. "What if my fans really like your flow? Decep Records will then have no choice but to let us make an album together. *The two finalists coming together to put aside their rivalry for the sake of music.* That's a headline right there. Through that, we would end up touring the world together. Both living our dreams . . ."

Isaac couldn't hold his grin back. Luke had always been so optimistic with everything he did. Maybe it was because he was so talented and gotten use to winning . . . or tired of losing. Either way, he could have gone pro in basketball. All he needed was literally one punch to prove a point in boxing. And rapping. It was the least of the three gifts, but look how that turned out.

"Thank you, bro, but that's not my dream," said Isaac, "I'll pass."

"I can't believe this . . ." the celebrity couldn't understand why he was so annoyed by the answers. Whether it was because Luke wasn't use to being rejected these days, or because it was *Isaac* who was doing the rejecting? He didn't know.

"Maybe you just don't know that some people are willing to kill for a feature, never mind a whole album." Luke ran back to the drink he poured, but left it hanging in his hand, "Earlier on, some masked man tried to poison me to prevent me from performing for a few weeks. Before that, a girl practically begged me to listen to her mix-tape –"

"And did you offer *her* a feature –"

"No!" Luke finally chucked the liquid down, "Like you, all she wants to do is rap, Jesus! Jesus! Jesus! Till her eyes close!"

How amusing. There was no way Luke could have known about that song, never mind it being Isaac's ringtone.

"I don't see how me being annoyed is amusing to you," he poured another cup, "forgive me for believing in your talent to become a well known rapper. You can live your dream just like me, Isaac. Travel the world making music just like me. All you got to do is change your flow, it's that simple."

"Bro, I can name many C. H. H. artists that have the talent to do so, but I don't think it's that simple, Luke. I would be giving up my faith to promote what we call *evil*, just for the sake of money and fame," explained Isaac.

"You can just repent after you have everything –"

"Bro! I didn't come to argue with you," Isaac had to compose himself again, his blood boiled fiercely trying to make him forget the purpose behind the visit, "I came to apologize . . ."

This stopped Luke from having a fourth. What did Isaac have to apologize for?

The celebrity was speechless. This must have been how the critics, who wrote Luke Chase off, felt when the unexpected happened. Isaac could have waited for Luke to come to North City before approaching him. Instead, he travelled all the way to Fortuna Island. He came all this way to . . . apologize?

"Isaac –" started Luke, but he was interrupted by a knock on the door. The event manager entered straight afterwards, "Is now a good time?" his lips read.

The women, who couldn't wait to get a piece of the celebrity, stormed past the manager. A few took on Isaac as if he was an option. One would think that the music video for *So Enjoyable* was about to be made.

Isaac got touched in ways he would rather have his future wife do than them. He pushed himself away from the girls, but that resulted in giggles from the gorgeous women. One felt more attracted to his innocence like she wanted the reward of being his first.

"Ladies, please give me and my friend five more minutes," said Luke gently, "then *we* can party all night."

The women moaned and tried to convince him otherwise, but the event manager grabbed their attention with loud explosive claps. They couldn't hear his voice, but they knew what he would say. It was their cue to leave, or else . . .

Luke saw the models out while Isaac needed some water after such heat. He got a foam cup and found an open jug.

"Oh, man, those were some beauties." Luke took every possible second to admire the women leaving, "You know what I always say? A woman with no token is a woman not taken." He turned around, "Bro that ain't –"

Isaac spat the transparent drink out, "What is this?"

"Don't worry," replied Luke, "just know it ain't water, man . . ."

"Then why is it in an open jug?" asked a gasping Isaac.

"When I went to America, the laws stated that I couldn't drink, cause I'm not yet 21," Luke got spring water out of the fridge, "Nick came up with this plan which somehow worked, but just between you and me, I think he paid the officers."

Isaac gave off a strange expression, like paying officers weren't common, or was he not surprised by Nick's actions?

"This atmosphere is dangerous," he took a sip of the water and followed it with much more as if he was trying to flush the alcohol out of his system. "I need to say what I need to say and leave asap."

They put their drinks on the side as they took their seats.

"Here it is: I'm sorry for the past three years, Luke. I became distance with many people and I'm sorry that you were one of them. Life hasn't exactly been the same since my father's passing, but I've slowly come to accept it. I'm not using that as an excuse. I just sincerely came to apologize."

The celebrity sat back and took a deep breath.

"I'll understand if you don't –" added Isaac, but Luke lifted his hand to signal silence. Mr. Banner's death hit him harder than he let on. Only Nick knew that *that* was the reason behind the delay in the album release. Now wasn't the time for someone else to know, especially Isaac. He would probably go on and on about how Luke should have dedicated the album to Mr. Banner.

"Look, man, I accept your apology . . ." *Liquor.* The urge to take that fourth drink became stronger. "And I'm really sorry about what happened to your pops," said the celebrity, "he was a great man, and like a father figure to me."

"Thank you, bro, I appreciate your kind words," Isaac took another sip of water, "you know, he was really proud of the way we were dominating that tournament. No one could believe what was going on. Two Christian rappers entered the Rappers Behind Bars competition –"

"All thanks to your pops," Luke quickly added.

"Yeah, he really knew people in high places."

"Still though, no one can say anything." The celebrity reminded Isaac, "Getting us into the competition was all he did. I will never forget it, he made sure that we knew, regardless of him being the MC, the fans and judges didn't know he knew us."

"That was one thing: he loved a fair game," said Isaac, "and we went through that competition defeating opponents and spreading the Word all the way to the final. He was so proud that he gave us a rap from his old days to show how joyful he was."

"And he could rap on any beat, bro. Who knew he was in a band that made rap rock a thing?"

"A combination of my mom and father, the King and Queen of Rap Rock. At least, so they said . . ." concluded Isaac.

They shared a laugh in remembrance of Mr. Banner, "But times have passed, man, some guy named Ronnie Radke from Falling In Reverse has taken rap rock to a new level, including a band called, From Ashes to New."

"I didn't know you listened to rap rock," Isaac's tone peaked curiosity. "Is that a path you want to take going forward?"

Was Christian rap really the last thing on Luke's mind?

"Haven't given it much thought really," he took a sip from his drink, "but Nick thinks I'll be able to reach another type of audience, if I were to feature. As if *I* feature."

"What about coming back to Christian Hip Hop?" Isaac was hopeful, "maybe if I stayed in contact, you wouldn't have -"

"What? Drifted away?" asked Luke.

He had basically said it. There was no point in turning back now. "Yes, maybe you wouldn't have drifted so far away from your roots," Isaac ended the thought for him.

"Look, man, I'm going to be straight with you on this," Luke clenched his fists together trying to keep himself calm, "I appreciate you coming all the way to apologize, truly I do. But regarding the music I've made and going to make, that has nothing to do with you. Even if you kept in touch every day just to tell me I should change my flow, I wouldn't have changed it."

"So you fooled us into believing you were going to spread the Word through music?" Isaac asked a question he immediately regretted.

The conversation was finally flowing like a rehearsed freestyle, and then he had to ask such questions . . . Luke downed his drink out of sheer annoyance.

"No, I didn't . . ." the celebrity was hesitant with his words. Somehow. "I agreed to change my flow, Isaac. It had nothing to do with you. Nick had me freestyle before I took you on. He wanted to hear my bars about money, and no surprise, he loved it. I was told if I won, that's the flow they wanted," said Luke, revealing the reason why he was chosen.

"And your answer?" asked Isaac, even though he already knew it.

"Is it not obvious that I agreed with it, Isaac? I agreed with the terms then and there," Luke sat back and took another deep breath, reminiscing. "I didn't think I would win, to be honest. Not when I faced the person I was hoping not to all night."

Isaac's forehead wrinkled in thought, "Who were you hoping not to - wait . . . me?"

"Nah, the judges," he said sarcastically, "of course you, bro! I haven't once said I thought I was better than you. I just know how to make better decisions when it comes to chasing dreams."

"You call what you did, *better* decisions?" said Isaac, offended.

"Look, man, I didn't mean it like that, but you yourself said that you couldn't impact the industry the way I did. I changed my flow, and look how it changed my life. I suggest you do the same."

The ladies entered the room, a few seconds early, eager for action.

"I want you to think about it," Luke stood up and pointed towards the open door, "just know, my door will be open when you finally make the right decision."

The Gospel Rapper stood his ground, "I think you know I've already made the *right* decision." Isaac Banner saw himself out, "I'll see you in North City."

THE HIDDEN GENRE

SATURDAY MORNING

THE HIDDEN GENRE

NINE

NORTH CITY Mall was hit by a wave of customers exploring it for the first time. A couple of tourists entered the CBM store and Isaac jumped at the opportunity to hear the English language in its first form. But they didn't need help . . .

"You're welcome," the staff member returned the smile, "let me know if you guys need assistance . . ."

Ever since he reconciled with Luke, it was as if the whole world was off his shoulders. Like his lips had discovered teeth for the first time, now it wanted to reveal its discovery to every stranger that passed.

The last two nights had been more than productive, but without a doubt, finding out that Ruth rapped, topped them all. Her lyrics repeated over and over in his head. His own number one hit. Still, he tried to dissect it every time.

Lord, I've been reading that prison letters
I've been trying to rid these burden pressures

Isaac had been reading Paul's letters as well, and last night he finally got a huge burden off his shoulders. He only had one more, but as long as Ruth and Luke didn't know about it, it was weightless.

My family has done well while I lag behind
Lord, help me understand that You are beyond time

Isaac needed the reminder that all things worked together, as well. He tried to convince Luke to turn from his ways, but he knew to leave it in God's hands.

See, my sister became a famous detective
My mother got married around the same age
I wonder if I am to follow those steps
Or should I keep my feelings caged?

Ruth never pitched up that evening they were scheduled to record together. It didn't help that she hadn't sent a message either. It also didn't matter, especially since the power went out. Over the phone Mr. Rennells ensured Isaac that the switch must have tripped from too much power. It would therefore be best to record another day, which he agreed with.

Who was Isaac kidding though? It's not like he was there to record more than he was there to spend time with Ruth.

He finally left the building knowing he would only see her next week again. Isaac had so many questions. Maybe too many *personal* questions. Could anyone blame him? He needed to know what she meant by:

Should I keep my feelings caged?

What feelings was she questioning?
"Hey, mate, I wanted the –"

Lord, when I lost her, I felt like my life was done

When she lost *her?* Who was this female, and why was she so important to Ruth?

"Sorry, sir -"

Now I like this dude with the same name as Abraham's -

And . . . does she like, *like* like -"

"Excuse me!"

Isaac snapped out of his thoughts, "Yes, sir, sorry, uhm, do you need help?"

"Yes, I do actually. S.O.'s new album, Augustine's Legacy, do you lads have it?"

"Yes, we do," Isaac guided the man towards the section, "I really enjoyed this album, sir. I must say some songs will make you start dancing out of nowhere."

The man liked the thought of it, "My daughter asked me if I have heard the album before, but look at this," he gestured to all the CD covers, "how am I to remember all these names? Anyway, I just need to see the cover, mate, I'll know whether I have listened to it or not."

"Okay, here we are," Isaac took a turn and grabbed the CD, "is this what you looking for, sir?"

"This looks familiar," he took his time thinking about it, "unfortunately, I think I've heard this one already, mate. But then again . . ." the customer looked excited to try something new, "Heaven On Earth by Hurt?"

"I honestly don't know if it's pronounced Hurt or H. U. R. T.," said Isaac, "but this is one of the albums that hit hard."

"Okay. And who are these lads?" he enquired next.

"Oh, that's Selah The Corner, Sevin, and this here is Bumps INF," said Isaac as he handed the customer several albums.

"Okay. And who would *you* recommend?"

"I would recommend all of them."

"Well, then it's done, isn't it, lad?"

"Great! Just like S.O., their rap music requires deeper thought to understand," said Isaac, "if you would like more options though, I can always show you our new releases."

"No, no, don't you worry, lad. As long as they are not mumbling, I will be fine with these. Thank you very much for your help," replied the customer as he made his way to the counter with the albums in hand.

+++

The store was hit with that sudden wave of customers only people who worked in a bookstore would understand, but it died down eventually and gave Isaac the opportunity to go sort out the new releases.

"Who would put KB's old CD here?" he spoke to the albums like they were little children of God, "we are waiting for the new album, it's only coming out later this month," he took it off the shelf, "putting the old one here won't make it new."

"Today We Rebel," came a familiar voice, "sounds like something I'm about to start doing."

Isaac responded with a mischievous grin.

"I don't like that grin on your face," admitted Luke. "Are you up to something?"

Isaac grabbed Bizzle's latest album.

"No, I'm just . . ." his lips read.

Luke's forehead wrinkled in thought, "Just?"

The Gospel Rapper pointed at the words.

"The Messenger? Oh! You *just* The Messenger," said the celebrity, reading his actions.

"Nice," his lips read again.

"Bro," Luke started to panic. The officer said they would clear all the drinks, how did they miss the one jug that Isaac used? "Is your voice gone?"

Next, Isaac grabbed Eshon Burgundy's latest album.

"Answer me –" Luke started to get agitated.

"My voice is fine, bro. Relax." Isaac put his finger on the cover, "Let's continue."

"For the Love of Money," Luke read carefully.

"Is what you base your decisions around."

"You know I got that love for money. Man, look at this," the celebrity moved the gold shinning shades, from his face, to hang from his jacket rather, "only money can buy this. But I like this game, what you got next, bro?"

Isaac picked up Datin's latest album, "What you need to realize is that . . ."

Luke glared at the cover. It wasn't hard to see where Isaac was going with this.

"I need to realize that it's volume one," he said sarcastically, "so from now on, you want me to keep an eye out for volume two?"

"You need to realize that C. H. H. Ain't Dead," Isaac put the album back, "when the living Word is being spread."

That was the line from the rap Yahshuandi, the Gospel Rapper, used in the final.

"Look, man, can't we just have a normal conversation without taking shots at each other?" Luke had to compose himself this time, "Cause that's what I came here for. I came to apologize for trying to make you choose between your faith and music. I see now that you want to represent your faith *through* music. And I respect that, bro, I really do."

"And I accept your apology," Isaac's smile seemed rehearsed. Luke called him out for it, but Isaac continued, "It's not that, I knew that *you* knew I made the right decision."

"And that's why last night, you said you would see me in North City. You knew our conversation would play over and over in my head . . . you used my overthinking to make me come to the conclusion myself," Luke finished off.

"And so you have figured it out?" replied Isaac, "I'm just glad the brother I knew is still inside that body somewhere."

Luke's eyes rolled around his head.

"And we'll find him in due time," Isaac patted Luke's shoulder when he walked past him, "trust me, bro. We'll find him."

+++

"I like what you guys have done to the store though," Luke browsed around, "it looks good."

"CBM represents nothing but quality," replied Isaac, "we're glad you like it."

"It's been three years, bro," said the celebrity, "I've long forgotten what CBM stands for."

"Nice one," Isaac laughed thinking Luke was being sarcastic, but when he realized that he was not, "wait, you serious? *Content* through *Books* and *Music*, bro. How did you forget that?"

"I don't know to be honest, but I'll never forget your pops' words, 'Books is more than ink on paper, like Music is more than words, my son. Looks would scare if you could see deeper, like Rubiks' seem complicated at first . . . until you solve one,'" Luke regurgitated in verbatim.

Isaac couldn't understand how Luke could remember that, and still convince himself that music was *just* an art?

"I got a question," Luke picked up a sale book, "I remember that the store is connected to the church, won't it be more convenient to have it all at one place?"

"It would but –" Isaac was cut off.

"We bought that building for the worship of God, not to make money through it," Mrs. Rennells entered the store and Luke's face went pale. "The Church gathers there for Bible studies. However, we do have services on Sundays and you welcome to join if you not busy," she added.

"Thank you. I will give it thought, Mrs. Rennells." Luke covered his mouth with the book and whispered to Isaac, "I don't think she likes me, bro."

"Plus, if you were really *that* interested in understanding the Kingdom, you would make the time to come to the store like you make the time to go buy food," she wasn't referring to Luke directly, but he sure felt like she was, "your spirit needs to eat as well, you know."

"I understand what you mean," he put the sale book back as if he would be forced to buy it since he "read" a page already. "Thank you, Mrs. Rennells."

"You're welcome," she completely flipped from all serious to smiling like a fan girl, "enjoy your stay . . . oh and Luke," she gave the girls giggling a quick glance, "please try to not make any of my staff pregnant." Mrs. Rennells turned to Isaac, "I'll be in the back room if you need me."

The celebrity's eyes followed the manager all the way to her destination. Once Luke was fully sure he could speak without her eavesdropping, "Bro . . ." he turned to Isaac, "what did she mean by that?"

The CBM staff member guided Luke's attention towards the culprits, "That's what she meant, bro." The girls sent shy waves in the boys' direction, "I can guarantee you my colleagues ain't waving to me like that."

Surprised at the distance they kept, Luke waved back. However, he wouldn't be surprised if their manager had a deeper meaning by what she said.

"Mr. Chase," Isaac left while the celebrity was distracted and returned with a professional attitude and another album in his hands, "since you are a customer, why don't you buy this independent album called, *Jesus Lives* by upcoming artist Luke Chase?"

"Upcoming artist?" the celebrity chuckled, "I can't believe you still have this, bro," he replied, genuinely surprised to see it again. "Is there any chance that you guys perhaps have this *upcoming* artist's latest album?"

"I don't think so, but I'll check on the system to be sure," Isaac turned around and immediately saw Ruth, "hey, you'll never guess who's -"

"Isaac, this album's trash. I wasted nearly an hour of my life," said Ruth, harshly. "Luke! Chase! Conquer! is nothing but pride and foolishness put into words."

"I'm sorry to break the news to you," Isaac turned to the celebrity behind him, "but it looks like we don't stock your latest album, Mr. Chase."

TEN

LUKE HADN'T seen Ruth in three years, but it was obvious she gained the pros and cons of a rose. "It's good to see you too, Ruth," his voice shivered in shock.

"We have a surprise visit from a celebrity today," said Isaac, trying to subdue the awkwardness, "I'm sure you recognize him from our younger days?"

Ruth gave the celebrity a thorough look, from head to toe and toe to head. Directly into his eyes, "No, I don't recognize him. Isaac," she turned to her colleague. "Who is this?"

"You got to be joking –" Luke said, almost offended.

"It's Luke Chase," Isaac added to the celebrity disbelief. "How do you not recognize him?"

"Oh, I know who Luke Chase is," she gave the celebrity another glance, "but *this* guy seems a little obsessed with jewellery. The Luke I knew never liked jewellery, because he thought it made people targets."

"That person clearly never had access to the type of jewellery that Luke has now," said the celebrity, "therefore, maybe your friend was just hating on those who did have."

"I don't think that's the case, because he never glorified guns nor drugs and he knew that those who did that . . . they were the ones with the jewellery in the industry," retorted Ruth.

"Yet this friend of yours didn't glorify guns or drugs to get all that he has," replied Luke, "so I don't know what your problem is with him."

"Okay, guys, that's enough," Isaac stepped between them like a referee before a boxing match. "Let's not have this in front of the customers, especially when the manager's here."

"My mommy's here?" asked Ruth, a little surprised.

"Yes . . ." Isaac replied, knowing their relationship was not that good.

"Okay," Ruth took a few steps back, "I'm sorry . . ."

"I accept your apology," said Luke.

"I was apologizing to Isaac –"

"And I was accepting on his behalf –"

"Guys!" Isaac got fed up.

The three were quick to shut their mouths when the back room door opened slightly.

What was this tension between them anyway? It's like Ruth saw their friend in a completely different light than she did when they grew up together. But then again, if any of Luke's songs were as bad as *So Enjoyable*, which was the only performance Isaac got to see, then he understood her frustration.

"Don't you only have a shift next week?" he tried to change the topic.

"Yes, but I wasn't expecting us to have a guest today," said Ruth, "so I thought I could come share my thoughts on the album with you. You know, have you listen and see for yourself how far our friend has drifted off."

"When you messaged that you were coming in," Isaac's voice peaked disappointment, "I thought you would come in personally to give a reason why you didn't pitch up the other night. You know, at the studio."

"Oh, wow, about that –" Ruth started.

"Are you guys still using the store room as a studio?" asked Luke, amused. He and Ruth had discovered the effectiveness of the store room by accident. The thick walls' kept all the sounds and secrets to itself.

"So what business is that to you?" replied Ruth. When she received nothing back, she faced Isaac, "Can we please speak about that another time?"

An agreement was made and Isaac would soon learn something he never thought Ruth would be involved in. Whoever warned people about the quiet ones, their warning was no different to the boy who cried, *wolf.*

"Just so you know," Isaac spoke to his colleague, "Luke likes what we've done to the store."

"Oh, wow, you said my mommy's here, right? I think I need to ask her if we can rearrange the store," said Ruth, still upset.

"I don't think that will be necessary," said the manager. She turned to the celebrity, "Thank you, Luke, we've worked very hard to get the store to the way it looks today. We happy to hear such positive feedback." Mrs. Rennells looked at her daughter, "Right, Ruth?"

Ruth stood firm in her stubbornness. She couldn't understand how her mother would take Luke's side after what he had done to her three years back.

Isaac stood there just as quiet as her after he heard *mommy* and *Ruth.* Those were known forbidden words in the Rennells' family. What changed?

"You know deep down," the manager looked deep into her daughter's soul, "that that is not the way we treat people, never mind customers."

Ruth had a war within herself, she couldn't process what was happening. However, what her mommy said was true. It turned the tide and made the good side win.

"I'm sorry for the words I've said today," Ruth gave the album to Luke, definitely not for an autograph. "No need to worry, I don't want . . . a refund won't be necessary," she left without waiting for any acceptance.

Isaac was tempted to ask Luke if he made a diss track or something.

"Don't worry about Ruth, I'll have a little chat with her," Mrs. Rennells spoke to the celebrity. "Are you too busy to join the Church tomorrow?"

Luke got put in the hot seat and his mind went blank. Not one excuse popped up, but that didn't mean he wanted to go. He hadn't seen a Bible in three years, never mind stepped into such a crowd of people.

"I will be there tomorrow, Mrs. Rennells," the words slipped off his tongue.

Ruth was upset with him, and Luke knew that he would see her there tomorrow. It was reason enough. He needed to find out what the real issue was. It couldn't just be the album. She was hiding something from him. But what?

"See you tomorrow then." The manager left, "Isaac, I'll be back in twenty."

"Yes, Mrs. Rennells," replied Isaac.

They watched her leave like children waiting for the go ahead to be naughty.

"Bro, can I get a lift tomorrow morning?" Luke asked Isaac.

"Nice one," Isaac laughed thinking Luke was being sarcastic *this* time, but then he again realized he was not. "Wait, you serious? Bro, I can't believe you forgot where the building is, as well."

"Come on, man," he protested, "it's been three years."

+++

Margarette tried to sleep the hours away, but it was always hard to find sleep when anxiety controlled the body. Tonight would be her first battle where the winner would get way more than what they put in. She wouldn't know who her opponent was until they were face to face. The rapper therefore had nothing planned. But that was fine, because freestyling was second nature to her. As long as she went second.

Margarette pulled up to the warehouse and allowed the car to do what she couldn't do earlier. The parking lot that she and her best friend stepped into was filled with cars, but the owners were nowhere in sight. Loud sequenced banging was coming from a single spot and they used that as a guide to the entrance.

"Remember, this isn't a street battle, Kane," said Gabi, "they have different rules here, something called, Eight Claps."

"They sure stole that word from the streets," Margarette commented.

"What do you mean? Don't they mean a clap? Like this," she gave an example, "that type of clap?"

"No, it's none of that *if you happy clap your hands* type of clap," Margarette used her fingers to issue her example, "it's that death type clap."

"They not going shoot *us*, are they?"

"Thanks for coming to support me, Gabi," said the rapper as she entered the warehouse.

"That's not an answer, Kane!" she chased after her friend.

+++

The place was packed with people thirsty for bars, drinks and apparently Gabi as well. On stage, there was a separation as if the two groups were about to compete in a dance battle.

"Last two opening acts before the main event," said a man before he spotted Margarette in the crowd, "and we have a new comer tonight, ladies and gentlemen. Also, I promise she go leave someone dead tonight."

The crowd reacted like this was the Roman Colosseum and death was welcomed. No, more like it was encouraged. The man gave the mic to another MC to start the next battle. Two female artists stepped up to face each other from the groups. Each staring the other down in disgust to share the stage with them. Then a beat dropped and the rap battle began.

"Yo, Kane!" the previous MC approached Margarette. "You on after this battle, you ready?"

"I'll be ready after you explain the rules, Joe," replied Margarette, straightforward.

"And why we got searched when we entered?" added Gabi.

"So the answer's pretty easy: we don't allow weapons in here," he spoke simple English to guarantee he won't need to repeat himself, "especially guns."

"Why guns particularly –" a shot went off and Gabi's heart rate found the sky.

"Relax . . ." Joe spoke soft to the girl who searched for exit signs, "I need you to relax."

"How can you tell me to relax?" Gabi shouted.

"What's your name?" he asked her.

"Gabi – my name's Gabi –"

"Okay Gabi –"

"We need to get out of here before we get shot –" panic overflowed in her body.

"No one's getting shot, Gabi," said Joe. "That's not a real gun shot. Look around," he gestured to the crowd enjoying the performance, "no one's running because they know it's not real."

Another shot went off.

"There again!" Gabi shouted.

"And again, no one's running . . ." Joe calmed her down.

"Just remain calm, Gabi," said Margarette with a reassuring hand on her best friend's shoulder, "there's nothing to worry about."

"It's just a sound used by the DJ over here," added Joe. "There's *really* nothing to worry about, okay?"

Gabi nodded. She understood, but her body would try jumping out of her skin more times than she could count by the end of the night.

"Rules?" asked Margarette.

"Okay, it's called, Eight Claps, but no one has ever gotten hit by eight before," explained Joe, "the crowd but mostly the DJ decides whether the line is hard enough to be a shot, and the one who gets hit the most, loses."

The current battle on stage ended 4-2 to the woman on the left that made baggy clothes look sexy. The loser, in a pale grey outfit, coughed up a good chunk of cash and walked off with her mouth on the floor.

"The next battle shall begin shortly," said the current MC.

+++

Joe took his place on the stage with Margarette and Gabi to his right and no one to his left. Where was her opponent? Had she gotten nervous and bailed, or was a lack of money the reason? Joe went to speak to the organizers for confirmation. This took time and the crowd got impatient.

"Skip this battle!" came a voice.

"Go to the main event!" pushed another.

"I promise you she's worth the wait," said Joe in the mic, not doing much to convince them, "just give us a minute –"

"I'll battle her," said someone that the crowd recognized immediately. They all froze as if he was the police, "If she is as good as you say she is, then she wouldn't mind facing a man for double the amount she put in."

Was this guy naturally confident or one of those cocky ones? For double the amount of money she put in, it didn't matter which one he was to Margarette.

"Just give me a minute," said Joe. The MC came closer to the female rapper and put the mic behind his back, "Kane, this guy has a serious hatred for women rapping and he's not ashamed of it. He'll make this battle beyond personal."

Margarette didn't waste her whole day being nervous, just for her battle to be swept under the mat in general; never mind some personal opinion.

"Come on, woman!" yelled the man ready for action. "You wanna battle, or not?"

Margarette looked at Joe, "Let me teach him some respect then."

It was about time someone stood up to the guy. He needed a good slap across the face and Margarette was the perfect person for the job. Joe gave her a *make me proud* smile. "We got a battle, ladies and gentlemen!"

The crowd got amped. Both rappers were given mics to introduce themselves.

"Ladies first," offered the opponent.

"Age before beauty," she replied, which got the crowd animated.

The DJ started the beat and Joe gave the guy the first go. He felt no need to introduce himself, but to respect the game, the rapper said that they were about to hear flames from the artist named, *Spoil T.*

"More like *Spoiled Brat*," mumbled Margarette under her breath.

THE HIDDEN GENRE

(Spoil T)

So you the one I heard that's a Christian?
Well, I don't believe when I speak, God listens
I don't feel the Holy Spirit nor hear a voice
Heaven or hell? Man, what a choice
!
No one owns me, I'm in control of my life and this rap battle
You nothing but someone's future wife that must obey like cattle
!
The universe like my rap started with a Big Bang
!
I'm the reason why God first created man
!

Cheers went all around the arena. Four shots was a mountain to climb in a contest like this. No one had ever received five before.

"Why are they cheering for him?" the opponent glanced at her best friend, "he completely contradicted himself."

Gabi didn't hear one and therefore lifted her shoulders as a *I don't know* response.

The instrumental zoned to the background to let Joe speak after the crowd applauded for Spoil T. "Okay, okay, we got four shots, ladies and gentlemen! Four shots. Will the new comer *rap whack* or *clap back?*"

"Rap whack!" yelled majority of the crowd.

Spoil T's head began to swell.

"Okay, okay. I see, we underestimating the new comer tonight," the MC said into the mic.

Surely Joe would call out the contradiction.

"Are you ready new comer?" he asked instead.

"Wait," Margarette stole the attention. "Are we going to ignore the fact that this guy just contradicted himself?"

Most of the crowd was confused, but Joe knew what she meant. Yet he was troubled looking at the VIP section for guidance. However, his eyes came back with confidence like he ignored his concerns, "Care to explain to us?"

"Yes! First he said that the universe started with the Big Bang, and then he says *he* is the reason *God* created man. These statements contradict each other because the prior happened over millions of years out of nothing. But God created everything in six days and rested on the seventh. Huge difference. If you ask me, he just shooting blanks."

The crowd liked the new girl's spunk. Her argument was concrete, based on facts. Joe went to discuss this with the DJ. They changed the amount from four to three shots.

Spoil T's head began to swell more, but with rage this time.

"Okay, okay. I think I need to pose this question again," said Joe, excited. "Now . . . will the new comer rap whack or *clap back?*"

"Clap back!" yelled the crowd.

"What crap is this?" the opponent finally spoke up, "that question never gets asked twice!" Spoil T looked at his opponent, "and we came to battle, not to decode words, woman!"

"Then let's battle!" Margarette stepped forward, "I go by the name, Mkay, bring the beat back!"

(Mkay)

Oh, so you went and made this battle personal
Now it gonna hurt more when you get schooled by a female
!
So you got no, "If God is good, could he remove all the evil,
please?"
The fact that you still here shows how merciful He is
!
Listen to me carefully when I say this, it matters which one you
choosing
Do I believe Evolution is false? Yes, and that the Big Bang wasn't
God's doing
!
In the beginning God created the heavens and the earth, rested
after the sixth day of work
I'm chosen strong, created from bone, you came from dirt
!!

The crowd lost their minds. Some cheered. Some laughed as the loser walked off. It wasn't announced yet, but everyone knew who the winner was. Maybe now Spoil T would think twice before being disrespectful to women.

"Our winner tonight?" asked Joe, "first woman to ever score a double shot, the new comer, Mkay!"

The people applauded cheerfully.

+++

Outside the warehouse.

"Yo, Kane," Joe approached her, "I can't believe you called Spoil T out for contradiction. No one has ever done that before. You killed it tonight!"

"Thanks, Joe! So I'll see you at a different location next week?" asked Kane.

His face expression did a complete 180 degree, "Check it out, as much as that was dope . . . the owner didn't like it, Kane. He thought it was disrespectful."

"What? I just pointed out the guy's mistake," Kane replied in defence.

"I said the same thing, but I don't own the place," said Joe, "I'm sorry, but he doesn't want to fund a rapper like you."

"A rapper like me?" asked Margarette. "He doesn't want to fund a rapper like *me*?"

"That's his direct words . . ." Joe reiterated.

"This industry just ain't for a rapper like you." Luke's words played in her mind again.

"I know it has nothing to do with you, Joe," she said, "don't stress about it. I'll find another place."

"If you really want to make money in battles, try the courts up city, but remember those are street battles. The cash is good, but defeat the wrong person in front of their crew, and that can be a big mistake. Plus, they don't point it out, they just point and pull triggers," Joe advised.

"I see what you did there. Thanks, I'll consider it," she got into the car where Gabi was waiting, "thanks for the night, Joe."

"Bye, ladies!" Joe waved as he went back into the building.

What Margarette Kane didn't expect, was that her first street battle in the courts, would be her last.

SUNDAY MORNING

THE HIDDEN GENRE

ELEVEN

A SIGN board was deep rooted into the grass. The saying was just as deep in the hearts of those in the Church. However, it was a new adjustment from when Luke was last here. The clothes he wore was black and plain. The hoodie was the perfect choice in case he needed a quick escape.

Questions. A lot of questions was what he didn't have the energy for, especially since his knowledge was at a minimal. Last night, Luke went through the first book in the New Testament like a student the night before an exam. Not because he had an interest to learn, but if questions were to start flying, he didn't want to look stupid in front of Ruth.

"Welcome to North City Church: This building is nothing but four walls without the Church," he read softly. "What happen to the days when we said, 'We going to church on Sunday,' not, 'The Church is meeting at the usual spot today,' it makes the church sound like a living . . . thing."

He dared not say *body.*

A hand planted itself on the celebrity's shoulder, "How dare you, Luke? How dare you stand with your shoes on sacred grass? Take them off!"

"What? Really? I'm sorry!" Luke almost panicked, "I will . . . but, you got yours on too."

"I'm just joking, bro," Isaac and his mom got a good laugh. "You said you went through the Bible last night, did you read anything about sacred grass?"

Question number one and already he had no answer. Luckily Ruth was nowhere to be seen. This was going to be a long service. Some of the older people looked at them as if they were little children making a noise. Luke felt an urge to go shove his awards down their throats.

Mrs. Banner saw Chantal with her daughter and took leave towards them. The "kids" greeted the latter with waves, but Ruth came directly to them. She hugged Isaac first. Luke thought that maybe the best was kept for last, but the first hug lasted longer than it should have.

"Welcome Luke," Ruth gave him a hug so short, one would think she friend zoned him, as if *Luke Chase* got friend zoned by women. "I'll keep seats inside for you guys."

Ruth hurried a bit to join a couple of the CBM staff members walking inside.

"And here I thought I've figured women out," Luke mumbled to himself.

"Thought no one would notice you with a hoodie on?" Isaac walked ahead laughing, "maybe she just recognized the Luke Chase that has no jewellery on. You never know, bro."

+++

Inside the seating seemed simple enough to everyone. But no one knew the war that went on at that very moment. Ruth left two seats on her left open, but left the decision in their hands. Isaac didn't want to be too obvious, so he gave Luke first pick. He had to decide if he wanted to sit next to Ruth and finally find out what her issue was, or get the last seat on the edge? No brainer . . .

He used the hug received as a guide to his decision and they finally took their seats next to Ruth. She sat next to the couple of CBM staff members, not too far from stage nor too close to it.

Luke showed enough respect to take his hoodie off once he was seated. Isaac was alongside his crush, and this gave Luke the end seat in case a quick escape was needed.

"Man, this place ain't as full as it use to get," Luke's eyes wondered around. "Bro? Ain't that the judges?"

Isaac stopped his conversation with his fellow colleagues the moment he heard the word *judges.*

"The judges from the competition?" Isaac asked.

"Yeah, I never took them for *Christians,*" said Luke, "I wonder if I should go greet them?"

"First of all, they weren't followers back then. They only truly surrendered their lives about six months ago," said Isaac, "secondly, we about to start. You can greet them afterwards, bro."

"But they are part of the reason why I am where I am today," replied Luke.

"Why do you say that?" Isaac questioned cautiously, "they did nothing but say who won and lost. What else could they have possibly done to get you to the place you are?"

"That's just it: I won, because on the day, they thought I was better than my opponent," Luke dared not say *'you'* as much as he liked the sound of it. "If it wasn't for them, I wouldn't have gotten that contract. I think I should –"

"Good morning everyone," Chantal took to the stage, "and a very warm welcome to our guests on this overcast morning."

Maybe Isaac was right and it would be better if he went to greet them afterwards, especially since they were serving in the church. Luke sat down, "I'll wait till after."

"Let's welcome brother Ryan this morning," Chantal finished and the Church welcomed him with a warm applause.

"Good morning to you all," said Ryan, "leading up to today, I really asked the Lord to give me the right words to say. See, I understand how difficult life can be for the youngsters of today. They surrounded by all these people talking about how great life is when you live for yourself, and how you should *totally* go find yourself. Let me tell you this, finding yourself doesn't make you any less lost, unless you found yourself in the Body - may ye with ears hear," Ryan journeyed to the book stand on the stage. "'Go on a soul searching journey to find out who you really are,' they say. I say, the day you find out who made you, is the day you find out who you really are. But listen to what Paul wrote to the Philippians:

Therefore if there is any consolation in Christ, if any comfort of love, of any fellowship of the Spirit, if any affection and mercy, fulfill my joy by being like-minded, having the same love, being of one accord, of one mind. Let nothing be done through selfish ambition or conceit, but in lowliness of mind let each esteem others better than himself. Let each of you look out not only for his own interests, but also for the interest of others. Let this mind be in you which was also in Christ Jesus. Philippians 2:1-5 NKJV.

Overall, what is he saying? We need to be more like Christ. Not ourselves. That's why you see Jesus told us to deny ourselves, not find ourselves. You can go how many years on a soul searching journey to "find yourself," but if you don't find that self kneeling at the feet of Jesus, then you have searched in vain, my friend. One day every knee shall bow, every tongue shall confess, that Jesus Christ, *is* Lord. With that being said, I want everyone to turn their attention to Luke."

Luke's heart stopped. "Bro . . ." he turned his attention to Isaac. "Is Ruth's father really going to put me on the spot like that?"

Was this their plan the whole time? To bring him to the church, call him out for being selfish without actually knowing that he gives back, and then mock him in front of everyone for not being Christ-like?

Every word brother Ryan said went in and out of Luke's ears, but he sat there, eyes forward. He felt like everyone behind him had their eyes in his direction, which normally was fine when he had a mic, but not in a church. Being here made him . . . nervous.

Why didn't his body want to move? Why didn't it want to escape when this was the exact reason why he chose the end seat? He was glued to this destiny of sitting here, but he could still make the decision to leave at the same time. He couldn't do it anymore. The pressure filled his lungs. How dare they judge him when the Bible says, not to judge? He turned to confront the hypocrites, but their eyes were in their Bibles.

"So for all those who don't have Bibles with them," continued Ryan, "I'm reading from the *Book of Luke*."

Was this part of his imagination? How had he forgotten about the book of Luke? Surely it wasn't the overcast weather that clouded the celebrity's mind. Luke had forgotten so much the last three years, it was as if his home town was throwing all the memories back at him when he least expected it.

"Then all the tax collectors and sinners drew near to Jesus to hear Him. And the Pharisees and scribes complained, saying 'This Man receives sinners and eats with them.' So He spoke this parable to them saying, 'What man of you, having a hundred sheep, if he loses one of them, does not leave the ninety-nine in the wilderness, and go after the one which is lost until he finds it? And when he has found it, he lays it on his shoulders rejoicing. And when he comes home, he calls together his friends and neighbors, saying to them, 'Rejoice with me, for I found my sheep which was lost!' I say to you that likewise there will be more joy in heaven over one sinner who repents than ninety-nine just persons who need no repentance. Or what woman, having ten silver coins, if she loses one coin, does not light a lamp, sweep the house, and search carefully until she finds it? And when she has found it, she calls her friends and neighbors together, saying, 'Rejoice with me, for I have found the piece which I lost!' Likewise, I say to you, there is joy in the presence of the angels of God over one sinner who repents.' Luke 15:1-10 NKJV.

Jesus went on to speak about the Prodigal Son. And I'm sure everyone knows about he who wasted his inheritance and still got accepted by his father when he returned. I feel called today to focus on these parables." He walked away from the book stand to face the Church. "I had three different dreams leading up to today, and in all these dreams, there was one main plot. This is what I believe it to be, but I admit that I could be wrong. What's going to happen is: the lost among us are going to be found, and our hearts will be tested just like the brother of the Prodigal Son. May ye with ears hear - Jesus came to save not the righteous, but the lost."

+++

The overcast weather threatened to let loose, but this didn't stop the two young men from stepping out from the covers of their heated car.

"Yo Claude, why are we here fam?" the man, who got out from the driver's side, asked. "I don't remember you saying that you have family in this part of North City."

"This is the place where the Rappers Behind Bars competition was held," came the reply, "Yahshuandi performed here in that final I heard."

"Did you hear that?" chuckled the man.

"What? What's funny?"

"It sounded like you said *Yahshua and I* performed here in that final *I* heard."

"That is how it's pronounced, right?" asked Claude, confused.

"Yeah, -"

"So I don't get what you trying to point out."

"Don't worry about it, fam," the man came to stand next to Claude. "More importantly, what's the plan?"

"I'm going to organize a concert and pray on it," he said as a cold wind cut through their jackets. "If he had some sort of social media platform, I could have gotten his number so easily, but he doesn't. So I'm trusting he heard the song that the Lord put on my heart and he shows up for the show. I think it's a good idea. Any thoughts?"

"What I'm thinking?" asked the man. "DJ Johnny and C:map are about to bring some heat to this city."

+++

The service ended before Luke got too uncomfortable. People started leaving as if they couldn't wait for it to finish. Others stayed longer to talk with people they hadn't seen whole week, but to them, they acted like it had been years. The chattering was deafening as one could hardly eavesdrop on anyone's conversation.

Luke was left out. It was no different from being at your best friend's party and not knowing anyone else. Plus, the fact that no one was talking about him just made it worse. He spotted one of the judges, from the competition, walking to the store room, "Bro, where's the bathroom?"

"Close to the entrance," said Isaac. "Don't tell me you forgot, 'Men to the left, because women are always right,' as well?"

"Nah, I remember," he lied.

Luke put his hoodie on and kept his eyes on the person next to him. It seemed like Isaac didn't want the celebrity to speak to the judges, so he would have to find a way to find out why, even if it meant lying. Luke kept his eyes on Isaac, trying to make sure he wouldn't be seen going to the store room instead of the bathroom. Hastily he got off the chair and turned in time to knock a woman to the ground.

"I'm really sorry . . . here, let me help you up," Luke offered a hand up after they gathered the woman's things. He recognized her from the Grand Fortuna Arena. It was the one with the cross on her necklace, "It's you . . ."

The face expression she had was familiar to Isaac, very close to déjà vu, but not. That look of disappointment mixed with anger. He had seen it before.

Where had he seen it? On himself. It was how he felt the past six months before he reconciled with Luke. But why did this stranger have such eyes towards him?

THE HIDDEN GENRE

TWELVE

MARGARETTE KANE gave Luke time to process who was in front of him, but it was futile like trying to score against a football team with a bus driver that was good at parallel parking.

"I'm starting to think you just like knocking people to the ground," she accepted the help up, "for a change, someone needs to knock some memories into you."

"That's only if they can manage to get a punch in," said Luke as people slowly took their focus off the situation, "and I don't mean to brag, but I'm an expert at boxing."

Considering who taught him how to defend himself, it was no surprise the celebrity was an expert, nor was the bragging.

"You must have had a great teacher then," she said. "Maybe I can meet - him? In the future . . ."

"I wasn't taught by a guy, believe it or not," came the reply, "I was actually taught by a girl, but I haven't seen her in a long time." He gave her the fallen items back. "It will be very difficult to organize a meeting, Miss . . ."

There it was: proof that Luke had forgotten her name after all.

THE HIDDEN GENRE

"You know, it's very rude to ask a girl twice for her name," replied an upset Margarette.

"If I swear there won't be a third time, would you tell me?" Luke charmed.

His smile brought warmth to her heart as it did back in their younger days. For a moment, she hoped that her name would bring a wave of remembrance over him. Not the woman he met at the Grand Fortuna, but the girl at the orphanage that taught him how to stand up for himself when he needed it the most. She knew she kept hoping against hope with the latter.

"Kane. Yeah, Margarette Kane, I remember now." Luke turned to Isaac, "She is the one I told you about, the one I met at the Grand Fortuna."

They exchanged greetings, regardless of the words that stung her heart. Would Luke ever remember her properly? Did it even matter anymore? Ruth watched everything play out from the background. Eyes firmly studying Margarette's every move.

"Can I call you, Marge?" asked Isaac.

"No, you cannot, or at least not around me," said Luke, with a hint of anger, "I only know one girl by that name."

He remembered! The girl from the orphanage, he remembered *her* name. Why couldn't he connect her face with it?

"And Kane is *nothing* like her," added Luke, which broke Margarette's heart.

He forgot . . .

"That name belongs only to one person . . .," Luke informed, "and she abandoned me."

Abandoned?

"Why would you –" Kane started.

"Don't ask me why she left please –" said Luke, over her.

"Believe that - Lukey?" the last word failed to make the jump from Margarette's tongue.

"Hey, Luke Chase," all eyes snapped towards brother Ryan as he stole the tension. "Don't you want to entertain us with a song from your album?"

A few members in the Church murmured in disbelief, but Chantal knew what album her husband was referring to. She got the CD, for the sound girl, in time to bring a wave of relief upon everyone. It was the album before the fame.

"Forever . . ." mumbled Margarette as she recognized the instrumental.

"Wasn't I trying to sell you this *Jesus Lives* album yesterday?" asked Isaac. "This is *forever*, does that mean all three of us will be performing?"

"Hope you still remember the lyrics," Ruth came closer and asked innocently, but because of the rift, Luke took it as a challenge.

"Why don't we find out?" he asked.

"Great!"

"I never thought I would ask this," said Luke, "but may *I feature* on the song with you guys?"

A smile tugged at Isaac's lips, "We would love for you to have your first feature with us."

Was Luke starting to humble himself?

"I still don't get it," they walked towards the stage when Ruth whispered, "we are the features on the album, not Luke."

"I'll explain later," ensured Isaac.

The tension disappeared as quick as it came. Margarette experienced a form of abandonment herself, but Luke's must have been worse. It was the only explanation for how he felt, unknowingly, towards her. She stopped at the exit point of the building. She couldn't leave when the beat was pulling her towards the stage, insisting that she take a stand . . .

A few fans whipped out their cameras as the three artists were given microphones. Mrs. Rennells had the sound girl restart the instrumental.

(Ruth Rennells)

You lift me up
I heard Your voice
Here I stand
I've made a choice
To live for You
Is what I'll do
Forever

As troubles come
To make me lose my way
Your Will be done
Even when the skies are grey
To live for You
Is what I'll do
Forever
Forever
Forever

Luke stepped forward ready to entertain the people in a way only he knew how. Some were praising the Lord, some were enjoying the track, and some had their eyes on him, to see if this was genuine, or another way to promote himself.

Would he freestyle new lyrics, or stick to the original?

(Luke Chase)

Living in a world where people worship fiction heroes
Living in a world with people: money hungry egos

Luke lost his voice and his mouth hung open.

Liquor. This was *his* lyrics? Had he predicted that he would slip into the world? How was he able to remember these words now, but not while he was falling deeper into the industry? *Liquor.*

Isaac put his hand on Luke's shoulder to calm the war within.

(Yahshuandi, the Gospel Rapper)

Life . . . To us, unpredictable
Christ . . . He is my foundation
Death . . . To us, inevitable
Christ . . . Showed His passion

Luke found his voice in the midst of the chaos in his head. He nodded in appreciation.

THE HIDDEN GENRE

(Luke Chase)

Jesus shared His love during my pain
Fighting my addiction of L's trying to gain
Enemies trying to kill my potential to grow
But I just continued to wish blessings upon them though
Thank you Lord for everything You gave
Thank you Lord for conquering the grave
I know that when I'm alone, it's You who cares
But I'm only human people, keep me in your prayers

(Ruth Rennells)

When I was down
When life seemed bleak
You gave me strength
When I was weak
So I'll worship You
And this I'll do
Forever

I've traveled far
And I've traveled wide
I've found Your love
Now I cannot hide
My worship of You
And this I'll do
Forever
Forever
Forever

(Yahshuandi, the Gospel Rapper)

Not everyone who says to Me
"Lord, Lord" shall enter the kingdom of heaven
But he who does the will of My Father in heaven
Many on that day will say to Me

THE HIDDEN GENRE

"Lord, lord, did we not prophesy and cast demons out in Your name?
Did we not do many wonders in Your name?"
And He will declare He never knew them
I'm awake now, but I searched for Him with rem

Margarette took to the stage with brother Ryan's mic. She used Isaac's next line, but turned the whole track into an unreleased remix.

(Mkay)

Forever Your kingdom be
Forever Your reign lasts
I tried to really focus on me
But without God I didn't last
I believed in this album, Chase
I swear you have a bigger purpose
Right now you trapped in a golden maze
But no matter what, the world can't contain this!

Isaac and Ruth couldn't believe their eyes. The videos were proof for anyone who refused to believe via word of mouth, whether there was fans, haters, friends or family in the building. Margarette Kane took shots at Luke Chase in front of everyone who stayed to witness. What did she expect to gain from it? His acknowledgement? His attention? His eyes? If that was the case, she succeeded. The celebrity acknowledged the rapper more now than ever. His attention and eyes were glued on her as she walked off the stage.

Looking back didn't cross Margarette's mind until after she left the building. A piece of her hoped to see Luke chasing after her, seeking answers, but all she got was raindrops.

Ruth saw the rest of the song to completion.

(Ruth Rennells)

You lift me up
I heard Your voice

THE HIDDEN GENRE

Here I stand
I've made a choice
To live for You
Is what I'll do
Forever

As troubles come
To make me lose my way
Your Will be done
Even when the skies are grey
To live for You
Is what I'll do
Forever

When I was down
When life seemed bleak
You gave me strength
When I was weak
So I'll worship You
And this I'll do
Forever

I've traveled far
And I've traveled wide
I've found Your love
Now I cannot hide
My worship of You
And this I'll do
Forever
Forever
Forever

The video of the performance went viral, or according to agent Dobe, the video of how Luke Chase broke his contract, went viral.

THIRTEEN

LUKE'S PHONE danced him awake, but he was no way in the same mood. *Money Goals* was his ringtone and his favourite song too, but it didn't sound as good when it forced his eyelids open, "It's Chase."

"Luke," the agent was raged. "Have you been on social media since you got back from the church?"

"No," his voice was still hoarse, "I went for lunch and then came to the hotel – "

"You know what, Luke? Being your agent doesn't mean being your mother. I don't want to know what you did after school. Just whether you have been on social media or not?"

What was Nick's problem? Why such an attitude at such a time in the evening?

Luke wasn't going to ask and risk the opportunity of sleep. All he had to do was answer questions and then listen to a lecture about social media. Nothing difficult.

"Nah, I haven't been on since yesterday, Nick. What's the fuss with social media anyway?"

"You're viral," boomed Nick.

"And you woke me up because . . ."

"This little stunt you pulled, this can cause you to lose your contract."

"What?" Luke rose from the dead and grabbed his laptop. "Hold up, what you talking about?"

"I'm sending you a link."

Luke saw the notification scream, *pick me*. It enlarged like his eyes when he saw the headline.

"*Has Luke Chase returned to his roots?*" Nick read the title. "Do you see it there in bold, kid? You actually performed in a church?"

The agent asked the question as if Luke could say, *no*, and then the video would disappear.

"I knew deep down that this was a bad idea," he continued, "but the CEO insisted that you wouldn't breach the contract. He had faith in you, Luke. Not that I don't, but I understand that you are still young and in need of guidance. I told him, he didn't want to listen, and would you look at this? I was *right* after all."

"Why didn't you tell me your thoughts from the beginning, Nick?" Luke got emotional.

"The CEO told me, he accepted the request because he wanted you to feel a part of the family; to know that we got your back. He had a good point. But now he admitted to it being bad judgement on his end. So due to this mishap, he wants you to return to the state before you bring more shame to the label!" Nick added.

"It isn't like that, Nick! They pressured me to perform . . ." the lie slithered off his tongue before he realized what he said.

For a moment there was no response from Agent Dobe, "Is that so?"

How was Luke expected to respond to that? With the truth? Nah, he already planted one foot in, what would a little white lie do now?

"Yeah . . ." Luke continued down his road of lies.

"Okay . . ." the agent opened a pack of cigarettes. Again, there was silence as if he was deep in thought.

"Nick?" the celebrity asked nervously.

Agent Dobe blew the smoke away, "I'm going to take your word on this one, kid."

A wave of relief knocked Luke onto his back.

"But you will have to override what you did earlier," added Nick.

"All good," said Luke, hastily, "I'm down for whatever."

"I may have to come North and organize you a gig before Friday's concert," said Nick, "we need to remind the people that you still on tour of your current album, regardless of the videos. A quick easy promo. We need to remind them that *you*, Luke Chase, *looked*, *chased*, and *conquered*. Sound good?"

"I like the sound of that," came the reply with relief sprinting throughout his body. "But what about the CEO though?"

"Don't worry about him, kid. I'll inform him about this new information and hear what he says," replied Nick, calmly.

"You want me to talk to him -"

"No -" Nick choked on the cigarette.

"You good?"

"I'm okay," the agent cleared his throat, "you don't get paid to talk, kid. It's my job to face those hard questions and talk on your behalf. You just be ready to perform at short notice."

"Thank you, Nick. I really appreciate this. I don't know what I would do without you."

"Don't mention it, kid," said agent Dobe, "just remember that the seven year contract is on the line here, don't forget that."

The phone was put down and Luke checked the time, "How is it only seven?"

The clouds had punished everything below with buckets of water. During that time he had lunch with the Banners and Ruth, the extra special guest. Luke hadn't felt that feeling of family in a long time, even without Mr. Banner's presence.

Who would have thought that the internet would cause so much "damage" during his trip to, and nap at, the local hotel in North City? Nick had to save the celebrity's career again, like he had to over two years ago, after the album was delayed.

Luke couldn't fall asleep with such adrenaline running through his veins. The sun may have been down and out, but the city was still up and about. His phone started bouncing up and down as if it wanted to party.

Unknown number.

Nick said to never answer these, but there was something familiar about the last three digits of this one. The name of the person was on the tip of his tongue. Curiosity won.

"It's Chase."

"Hey, it's Ruth."

Ruth? He hadn't spoken to her over the phone since he left the state, but Luke had no memory of ever deleting her number. In fact, with all the women he was around, he forgot all about her, so when did he take the time to get rid of her number?

"How did the unpacking go?" she asked.

"I didn't start to be honest," he admitted, "I dozed off the moment I got to the hotel."

"Oh, wow," Ruth was concerned. "You don't know about the videos then?"

"I do," he chuckled, "I actually just got off the phone with my agent about it."

"You don't sound worried though."

"Because I'm not."

"That's very good to hear," she said with a smile, "we are really proud of you, Luke. You, remembering your lyrics is a good sign, plus Isaac told me what you meant by asking to feature. I'm grateful to be a part of that . . . to be part of a moment with the Luke Chase I remember."

"Thank you, Ruth," replied the celebrity, "I'm grateful to have you by my side . . ."

To him, Ruth, may have been the loyal girl one kept guessing until the prime years was done, when it was then time to settle down with one woman.

"You already seem to have a female by your side," said Ruth, who tried to dig up information regarding his interaction with Kane.

"I don't think she's in the same boat as us," said Luke. He didn't want to talk about Margarette right now.

"Why? Cause she totally called you out?" asked Ruth, "I didn't think she could rap, never mind *battle*."

"What? Did you think you were the only female out here rapping?" asked Luke, jokingly.

"No," she giggled. Before Isaac, Luke was the only one who knew Ruth rapped. "And I definitely thought you would forget about something like that."

"I could never forget about you, Ruth."

There was no response. She wasn't going to go down this path, not again.

"Ruth?"

"I've only recently forgiven you, Luke," she finally said, "please don't say things like that - especially since . . . look, I don't want to go through this again, not now."

"Wait, did you just say you've forgiven me?" Luke was confused. Was this connected to the way she treated him at the store? He wanted to ask her then and there to explain, but this wasn't a conversation to have over the phone.

"Yes, Luke," her voice was firm. "You're forgiven . . ."

"Ruth -"

"Let's not speak about it over the phone, please," she said. "Maybe we can meet up some time in the week?"

"Sure," he surrendered, "let me know when you available."

Ruth was in the yard at Mrs. Banner's house when the back door opened. "I will message you. Bye . . ."

"Who was that?" Isaac asked coming out with two steamy hot chocolates.

"Luke."

"Oh, how's he doing?" he gave her the portal to chocolate heaven, "I won't be surprised if his agent gave him an ear full after seeing the videos."

"He said he just got off the phone with him," she took her first sip, "Luke seems okay with it, like he isn't ashamed at all."

"That's a good sign, right?"

"I don't know, Isaac . . ." Ruth stared at the cup like it was a crystal ball showing her past, "Luke doesn't sound like he remembers what he did."

"What makes you say that?" Isaac moved closer to comfort her after her tears answered the question; it was clear she wasn't referring to anything recent anymore.

"I never knew that our song was referring to both of us reconciling with him . . ." Ruth managed to say, "I mean, who would think of that?"

"Our Father did."

"Yes, He did," an evitable smile came upon her face. "I felt such relief when I finally forgave him Saturday night. It's amazing how God used my mommy to get through to me though."

"The last person you expected?"

"I'm closer to my daddy, so yes, I never expected my mommy to get through to me," Ruth slightly distanced herself as she sat up. She stared directly into Isaac's soul, but she still couldn't see it, "What did you forgive him for?"

Was now the right time to tell her? Return the favor? She had told him what happened between her and Luke. It was only fair he told Ruth what happened between him and Luke.

"It's not necessarily about forgiving *him*." Isaac broke eye contact, "It's more –"

"Ruth, your mother –"

Mrs. Banner stopped mid-sentence, she didn't know if it was necessary to ask the kids if they knew who they were pointing their dagger eyes to or not.

"I didn't mean to interrupt you guys," she said rather, "but Ruth, your mother's outside."

"Okay," Ruth was sure to finish her drink before she left. "Thank you for the lunch, Mrs. Banner. I really enjoyed our time together."

Isaac took the cup from Ruth and followed after, but Mrs. Banner ensured him that she'll see to tonight's dishes, "Walk her to the car, son."

+++

Outside, the smell of wet grass was reason not to take a short cut to the car. Soft rock music played through the speakers of the vehicle that Chantal kept warm in. The kids came out of the house, one by one, willing to go the long way round.

"Thank you for this, Ruth."

"This wasn't work Isaac," she replied, "no need to be formal. Yes, lunch, with Luke joining us, was great. But more than anything, I enjoyed the time we got to spend together. Maybe we can do this again in the near future."

She had taken the words straight out of Isaac's mind, saving him the effort of trying to word it himself.

114

Their mothers waved at each other. Their friendship made it easier for the young ones to have these gatherings, but harder for them to express their feelings for each other.

"Have a great evening further," said Chantal.

"You too!" came the reply from Mrs. Banner.

Their exchange made Isaac aware of the limited time he had with Ruth, where she was reminded of the unlimited time she wanted to spend with him.

"Sweet dreams, Isaac," Ruth put her chocolate scented lips on his cheek and left.

"You too . . ."

Her lips were wet on his skin. Isaac stepped back to watch her enter the car, but his heel slipped off his slipper onto the wet grass. The coldness traveled throughout his body like lighting, and likewise, he was into the house the moment Mrs. Rennells' car was out of sight.

"Can you believe this?" Mrs. Banner said to her son, almost in disappointment.

"Believe what?" he asked, slightly confused, "nothing really happened, mom."

"Exactly," said Mrs. Banner, "you're just as slow as your father."

THE HIDDEN GENRE

TWO
DAYS
LATER

THE HIDDEN GENRE

FOURTEEN

MORNING COULDN'T come quicker. Isaac sprang to life before the alarm on his phone did. After prayer, he spent the rest of the morning in the kitchen.

It wasn't mother's day nor Mrs. Banner's birthday, but she found the smile, the spotlight of her son's face, contagious. "You making breakfast?" she asked, curious.

"You better believe it, mom," replied Isaac placing the plate in front of her, "it's your favorite too."

"Bacon, eggs, toasted bread with viennas, *and* grilled mushrooms," she looked at him suspiciously. "When did you learn how to grill mushrooms?"

"Dad taught me a while back," whenever he needed something, "He said, 'It worked every time.'"

"What *worked* every time?"

"The way he grilled the mushrooms," said Isaac nervously as he grabbed a knife and fork.

"He sure taught you all right," Mrs. Banner accepted the utensils with a shy smile tugging at her lips in remembrance. Her late husband was everything she wanted in a man, even when he forgot certain details, "You know how I know? Because he always forgot that I preferred juice over coffee with this breakfast."

"I'm sorry about that, mom," he attempted at a stand. "Would you like me to get the juice rather?"

"No, don't you worry about it," she ensured him, "just because things don't go the way one prefers it to go, doesn't mean it's the end of the world, son. Now then, shall we eat this delicious looking food in front of us?"

Breakfast flew by as their mouths were filled with laughter and delicious food. Ivan Banner, her late husband, was a topic she avoided around her son, but today was proof that it no longer had to be that way. They could remember the happiness that the man brought them, rather than dwell on the sadness of missing him.

"Thank you for this, Isaac. I haven't had this much fun over breakfast since your father was taken."

"It's my pleasure, mom. I think we both longed for it."

"I think so too, son. I think so too," said Mrs. Banner, "now onto the discussion."

"Discussion?" he tried to sound as innocent as possible. " *What* discussion?"

"If the breakfast didn't give it away, then the point of your father saying it *worked* every time, did."

"So you knew this whole time?"

"Trust me, all parents seeing this play out, knew what was coming, plus, just so you know, it *did* work every time he did it," she confessed. "More importantly, what do you need to use the car for this time?"

Isaac had a playful smile. "It won't be for another trip to Fortuna Island, or anything on such a level. You see, C:map, that guy we heard on the radio, he's having a concert tonight, and I plan on inviting Ruth."

"Why don't you ask her right now over the phone?"

"Because father taught me: when you ask a woman straight to her face, look her in her eyes, and you'll know whether the reply is from the heart or not," said Isaac, red-faced, "he said he used it on you actually."

"I know he did," she laughed, the comfort of speaking about Ivan, without depression taking hold, continued to please her soul in places she didn't know mourned for him. "It's so old school, but did he tell you I rejected him that day?"

"What? No, he didn't. He told me that the incident confirmed that he was in love with you," said Isaac, "the confirmation you needed as well."

An uncontrollable smile came upon Mrs. Banner's face. "Maybe you are not as slow as your father, after all."

+++

Around lunch time, Isaac finally found the courage to approach Ruth about the concert. Throughout the day, he battled his fear of the, father like son, possibility, especially since his dad got rejected. Yes, according to the story, he got the girl in the end, but Isaac didn't know if he could wait a couple more years for what he wanted yesterday already.

"Guess who's performing tonight?" he played it safe.

"Who?" asked Ruth.

"C:map."

"Who's C:map?"

"You joking, right?"

She wasn't.

"He was the guy we heard on the radio last week," said Isaac.

Not convincing enough.

"He was guided to make the song about myself and Luke, remember the track, *Purpose For Living*?" added Isaac.

"Oh, wow, yes, I remember him now," said Ruth.

Finally.

"*He's* in North City?" she asked.

"Yes, so I was wondering if you and –"

"And I'm seeing Luke tonight . . ." Ruth was deep in thought. "I wonder what would happen if they "accidentally" ran into each other?"

"You seeing Luke tonight?" the sound of the question made Isaac sick inside. "Where are you guys going?"

Did he really want to know?

"Whether he's picking me up tonight?" she replied, "I don't know, but I get to choose the place. And I'm thinking, maybe we can go to the concert tonight."

Isaac's insides compressed. She stole the words right out of his mind, once again.

"I should return his message right now before I forget," Ruth pulled out her phone, "thank you for telling me, Isaac. I really appreciate this . . ."

Luke *messaged* her? Was his mom right about his dad's teachings being too old school? Regardless, how did the conversation turn from Isaac inviting Ruth to a concert, into him giving her an idea of where to go with Luke? It was like father like son, after all.

+++

Luke and the stars came upon them like a thief in the night. Chantal was still in the kitchen, while Ryan gathered with the Church at the usual spot. The knocks on the front door indicated that a patient person awaited.

"He's here already?" Ruth scrambled towards the windowsill to be sure. There stood a limo with a driver standing guard in the driveway, "That sure is him."

Luke knocked on the door gently like it was something precious instead of hooting from the driver seat. That was a good sign. But then again, he did get a lift here, so he was never in the driver seat to begin with. So maybe it wasn't. But then again, he could have asked the driver to hoot, but he didn't. So that was a good sign, after all. But then again . . .

"Ruth!" came a voice from within the house.

"I'm still busy getting done, mommy," said Ruth. "Can you please let him in?"

"Okay, but please don't be too long," replied Mrs. Rennells, surprised at why dressing took so long, "I want to finish the food before your father gets home."

Chantal opened the door to find Luke in a stylish suit. She welcomed him inside.

Did she miss something, or was Ruth lying about going to the concert? Last time she checked, a suit was not what a male wore when going out with a female *friend*.

"Ruth will be down soon, you can make yourself comfortable in the lounge so long," she guided him, "I'm busy in the kitchen, if you need something."

"Oh, don't worry about us, Mrs. Rennells," said Luke, "I'll make sure she eats tonight."

Chantal didn't like the way the words came out of the celebrity's mouth, but she trusted that he didn't mean it in the way his music did. Plus, her daughter learnt her lesson and wouldn't go down that path again. She hoped.

Women usually took a while to get done whenever they went out with the celebrity. A need to look just as good, he guessed. Luke was to relax on the couch until then, but there was something about the passageway that was more attractive. It reeled him in.

A wall of framed photos stood in his way. A brief history of the Rennells' family, aligned in order from what would be the best memories of every five, if not three years. Every family member he knew, except for the one girl he thought was Ruth at first, however, she didn't look nothing like the girl he knew as a young adult. A photo, that had her and Ruth with their parents, was confirmation that they were indeed two different people.

Why hadn't Ruth mentioned her?

"That's Casey," said Mrs. Rennells as if the celebrity had thought out loud, "she's my first born."

"I never knew Ruth had a sister."

"That's because Casey moved out long before you and Isaac met Ruth."

"But she also never spoke about her," said Luke, "she loved to talk about you and Mr. Rennells, but not once did she mention another family member, never mind an older sister."

He studied the images and they were smiling at him. Nah, they were laughing at him. He who got abandoned by his parents. He who never felt the love of his parents. But Luke became a famous rapper without them though. He never needed his parents. Still . . . why haven't they reached out? Deep down he wanted them to. If not for his love and forgiveness, at least for his money and status. But no, no one tried to claim him. It was strangely disappointing.

"Makes sense . . ." Chantal finally said, "our first daughter got a lot of fame for cracking cases. Ruth probably thought she was being ignored during all that." Mrs. Rennells was thinking out loud more than anything.

Was that what siblings were for, to be nothing but competition? Did he have a brother out there that could challenge his fame? Did he have a sister out there that could challenge his looks? Luke didn't know. All he knew was the orphanage, and that if he hadn't gotten into it, he would have been dead by now, or somewhere all alone in the streets. Luke didn't know if one was worse than the other at this stage.

His pocket shook like a creature was trying to escape. Luke took out the object and the agent's name appeared.

Agent Nick Dobe, the man who saw potential in him. As much as he was thankful to the orphanage, he may be equally, if not more thankful for Decep Records. They made him into the artist and person that everyone admired today. Where would Luke be without them? They were his real family.

"Are you going to answer that?" asked Mrs. Rennells.

"Yeah . . ." Luke snapped back to reality, "it's Chase."

"Luke, I need you to stop what you doing and listen to me. I'm going to give you the decision on this one, but you need to make the right choice and make it now. I've organized a gig for tonight, and it starts in an hour –" Nick rushed through his sentence.

"You can't be serious?" Luke was clearly not impressed and hated his plans being treated as second to his career.

"I very much am, but like I said, the decision is in your hands," said Nick, "however, please note, if you do not pitch up tonight, your contract will be terminated."

FIFTEEN

MRS. BANNER sat in her war room, not too far from the kitchen. She was digging into the scriptures and came upon the parables in Matthew. She got absorbed in it, everything around disappeared and left her alone with the Word of God.

Why was the Spirit leading her to the parables? Who would she reach with them? Surely God would reveal it.

A struggle at the front door startled her. It continued like the man who wrestled with God. Mrs. Banner slowly approached her room door as the front one gave in.

Was it Isaac? No, she hadn't heard the car pull up, plus, he was with Ruth tonight.

The intruder closed the door and another struggle with what should be fake keys took place. It was as if the door used it's last breath to hold off the enemy for her to escape. But Mrs. Banner did the opposite.

"Come on," a mutter came from the door as she approached cautiously with a weapon.

A weapon? When did she take the time to grab something? Mrs. Banner looked at her hands shivering and there it was, the weapon. She had grabbed the Bible for protection.

Since Isaac had the car, this intruder must've thought no one was home. The steps were heavy on the wooden floor; it had to be a male.

This guy also had to be really confident that no one would come home for quite some time, or really stupid to go have a meal in the kitchen before checking the house.

"Thank you, mom," the voice said to himself, "this is what I need right now."

Did this guy pray to a mother god? If so, how was the parables connected to it?

The moonlight, invading the house, revealed the figure of the man who sat by the table. The hairstyle, in the dark, familiarized itself with her. The cold stung Mrs. Banner's arms as she leaned against the wall. The pain would be worth it if she could endure long enough to get a final glance at the intruder. Luckily, the man prepared to use the knife and fork for her supper, rather than her. Then she found out why.

"Isaac?" she snapped the light on. "Why are you sneaking around?" the Bible relaxed on her side, "you nearly gave me a heart attack."

"I'm sorry, mom," he stood up in his reply, "I didn't want to wake you up . . ."

"It's fine, I wasn't sleeping –"

Isaac's eyes were drawn to the weapon, "Were you going to hit me with that?"

"What can I say? I thought you were an intruder, Isaac. I heard no car pull up, which I admit, is probably because I was full on focused in the Word, but still, that was scary, son."

A playful smile overtook Isaac's face. "So you were either going to hit me with the Word, or actually *hit* me with the Word."

"You'll be surprised what a hardcover book can do, just ask John Wick," joked Mrs. Banner. "Where did you park the car?"

"The car's outside," Isaac sat down, "I'll pull it in after I eat, if you don't mind."

"I do actually," she said sarcastically. "That's *my* supper."

"Oh . . . did you make me?"

"It's fine, you can eat it, son."

"You're the best, mom," Isaac left the elephant in the room and continued his mission with the food.

"I didn't think you would be home this early," his mom tried to pry and get an answer.

"It's okay, what were you reading though?"

The elephant felt ignored.

"The parables in the book of Matthew," she took a seat next to him. "But what happened today? I thought you were going to the concert with Ruth."

"No, she decided to go with Luke tonight," he said with nothing but disappointment in his voice, "I'm sorry I didn't let you know earlier."

"I don't believe you."

"What don't you believe?"

"I don't believe she *chose* to go with Luke." Mrs. Banner got the expected silence in return. "Isaac, did you ask her if she wanted to go with you?"

"No, but –"

"No buts, Isaac. If you asked her like you said you were going to, maybe you could have gotten your answer that your father promised you would get."

"How would that have changed the fact that she's going with Luke to the concert? They had planned to get together tonight, mom. How would me asking change that?"

The very fact that Isaac hadn't the slightest clue to the answer burned his chest. His stomach begged to be kept busy. Anything to prevent any thoughts about the situation. It was as if the elephant now sat on his shoulders.

"You would have learned that she's being a genuine friend to him right now," said Mrs. Banner, "Ruth isn't looking for someone like him to start a family with. She is looking for a man of God, not some kid enjoying the benefits of being famous. You know deep down that Luke needs our guidance now more than ever. Ruth is showing that she's there if he needs someone to talk to. You should prepare yourself too, son."

"Prepare myself for what?"

"For the day Luke comes knocking on that front door seeking advice."

+++

Terror was written all over the celebrity's face as he lowered the phone from his ear. He could understand the reaction if he did something drastic to destroy his reputation, but all he did was perform a song with his old friends. How did it become a situation that could cost him his career?

If he were to be terminated, it would be fine, wouldn't it? Luke Chase was famous, and many labels would beg for his signature. However, there was no guarantee he would get the exact same contract. Decep Records was nothing but good to him. He had to return the favor.

"Is everything okay?" Ruth asked coming down the stairs.

Her appearance made it hard for him to find the words to say. The hip hop outfit she wore revealed only her arms, neck and ankles, while she carried her jacket like a handbag on her forearm. This gave Chantal some relief. But Luke was overdressed.

"You ready to go?" Ruth asked as she saw Luke's facial expression.

"Did I make it in time?" Ryan entered the house.

"Yes, you did, daddy," Ruth answered.

"That's a very fancy suit, Luke," Ryan commented on the appearance, "I like it."

Ryan always focused on the good of the kid, never the bad. Chantal never understood it, even after what the celebrity did to their daughter, he still believed that Luke must have had a valid reason. Whenever she approached her husband regarding the topic, he always shrugged it off, "The kid would never get to meet his parents," Ryan said once as if he was the reason why, "I can't imagine what that feels like."

"Thank you, Mr. Rennells," said the celebrity, "yours is not far off."

"I mean, I try, but thank you," came the reply. "And you look beautiful, princess," said Ryan to Ruth before he kissed his wife and went to put his stuff down.

"What about me?" Chantal asked out.

"You too, honey!" Ryan shouted.

They shared a laugh as Mr. and Mrs. Rennells saw the kids out to the limo like it was their senior year dance.

+++

On their way to the venue, Luke gave nothing but one word answers. *Liquor.* Ruth couldn't take his distracted nature anymore.

"Are you going to tell me what's wrong, Luke?" she asked, "I heard you on the phone with someone earlier, do you want me to tell you now what I wanted to say later, or is there something you want to tell me first?"

"Nothing . . ."

She stood firm in her annoyance.

"We not going to the concert," he finally spoke in full sentences, "my agent phoned me, I have a gig tonight, and if I don't pitch up, the label will release me. Meaning I'll be living on the streets regardless of how famous I am."

"What happened to me choosing where we going?" Ruth asked in annoyance.

"Did you not hear what I said?" he snapped, "if I don't perform tonight, I will lose my contract. And right now, I'm not willing to risk that for . . ." he dared not say, *you.* "After the gig, we can go wherever you want to go. Okay?"

It was clear that this couldn't be negotiated. She accepted the terms and conditions in hope that her friend would use the opportunity to spread the Word. How foolish she was.

+++

They came to a club of a different kind, but it wasn't a sports club either. There were no lines filled with overexcited hormones. And there were only two bouncers at the door; but it was probably their size that forced that predicament.

Inside, the bass didn't drown the lyrics, but allowed the words to float throughout the place. Suits were everywhere like it was going out of fashion, and Luke would have blended in perfectly if it wasn't for the style of his. But Ruth was underdressed.

She wanted Luke to use this as an opportunity once and for all to get off the fence. Right now, he hung on it staring at the other side, as if the opportunity to climb back over were to present itself, he wouldn't think twice.

Was this that opportunity?

"Stay by my side," Luke put on shades to keep the ladies guessing when his eyes wondered around, "you don't want to be alone in a place like this."

Ruth stole many eyes, mostly women's, but they were daggers more than anything. Their eyes questioned what made her so special to be with the one and only Luke Chase? But all she really wanted was Isaac's gentle chocolate eyes, yet he was too oblivious to the signs. Luke on the other hand was too immature to be involved in a real relationship.

Why did she agree to this anyway?

"Luke!" yelled Nick Dobe, "I'm glad to see you, kid."

"I've come to do this gig and get back to my life, Nick," said Luke, seriously. "Nothing more, nothing less."

"That's what you get paid for, but I got to say," the agent checked his client out, "this suit is better than the one we prepared for you."

"Thank you, but this was for my date."

"Excuse me," Ruth interrupted. "Date?"

They were too close to the speaker for Luke to hear the tone of her voice properly, therefore he introduced her as if that was what she meant.

What the celebrity didn't know was that they knew each other already, not face to face, but over the phone, and this made the agent nervous.

"You go get ready, kid," said Nick, "I'll guide Ruth to the VIP section."

Luke Chase left and the agent stood there with his eyes studying Ruth. She was displeased with him as much as she was with Luke over the issue. Regardless, Nick offered his arm to the guest. "May I?" Because of Luke's warning, she accepted it. "Did he pick you up by your house? Are you the reason for that little performance at the church? What are you playing at Ruth?"

She need not answer what she didn't want to.

Nick was annoyed at her silence. "Are you trying to ruin this boy's career, *girly*?"

That was it, Ruth broke away from him as they reached the VIP section. Never once in the past two years did she think she would defend her mother as "owner" of that word. "You, more than anyone, don't have the right to call me such."

The incident caught the attention of a few VIP members. Nick hid the rage and portrayed a smile instead, "Just sit back, relax and watch the revival."

+++

Luke was backstage mentally preparing himself to perform for the crowd. "I got this!"

"Yes, you do," Nick added encouragement, "you're going to show them tonight why you are currently the hottest thing on everyone's lips."

"Where's Ruth?"

"VIP section."

"Alone?"

"No," he lied, "I left her with someone."

After some silence as if the celebrity questioned whether his agent was telling the truth, Luke accepted the answer. He admired himself in the mirror, "Hottest thing on everyone's lips? That depends on which tracks we going with."

"You'll know when the beat drops, which is which and why I chose it, but we going with your favourite first."

"I like the sound of that," concluded the celebrity.

+++

Ruth sat back like Nick told her to, but she couldn't relax, nor did she have any intentions on watching some kind of revival. She got up to get a drink, but nothing there would calm her down the way hot chocolate did. Something slithered on her shoulder, giving her a fright.

"Whoa," replied the man as his drink spilled. "Why you so tense, baby? You need to relax a little."

He offered her a drink that would do just that. But it wasn't her favourite form of chocolate, so Ruth didn't want it. "I'll spill that drink too if you don't get it out my face."

The man backed off like the current song. The crowd waited in anticipation for the next track to begin, but got disappointed when Nick stepped on the stage, "Guys, when you came here tonight, you were expecting to see some gorgeous women, *and* look around; you got what you wanted. Ladies, when you came here tonight, you were expecting to see some ugly men with deep pockets, *but* look around; you got exactly what you expected."

Nick got them laughing with some taking slight offense, but too ashamed to make it known, "Tonight," he continued, "I've managed to organize a performance from the recently named *sexiest man alive*! Let's give it up for Luke Chase!"

The moment the first sample of the instrumental jumped out of the speaker, it put Ruth too on edge to sit down. It was the song from Luke's latest album. It was Money Goals.

(Luke Chase)

Money - Goals
Dope - Flows
Broke - Hoes?
Ain't Got - Those

Money - Goals
Watch Me - Pose
Fake - Bros?
Ain't Got – Those

Ruth hoped against hope that Luke wouldn't continue. That he would realize the stupidity in the lifestyle he was promoting. That he would step off the stage regardless of how damaging it would be to his career. More than anything, that he would listen to her.

But Luke didn't even show a hint of hesitation as he let the music overtake him.

THE HIDDEN GENRE

(Luke Chase)

Wanted success to gain things I never had
Doing maths. No division, boy, we just add
I be stealing their loyals like a looter
You call me now cause you ain't got a future

They told me that money can't buy me happiness
But I feel really happy riding this wave of success
And I heard that I can't serve God and mammon
Yet how I made it? They just can't fathom
If wishes were fishes the whole world would be an ocean
If fishes were money - you'll have my bank account
Focus on what you got and haters - don't deal with them
Breaking so many records that I actually lost count
Homie came to the joint in a carbon lambo
Looking good - not some dude searching for a ho
Yeah I'm rich but that won't stop me from making more
Got green running through my veins to my core
Some be thinking that I may be god in the flesh
Cause I'm covered in gold and you see me less
I be making this paper and then found out it's cotton
Like the Messiah. Boy, I will not be forgotten

It was too much. Ruth couldn't sit, relax nor watch it anymore. She got up to leave and continued her journey until she was out of the club.

Luke's eyes travelled alongside her from beginning to end.

Liquor.

The crowd continued with the hook regardless of the frozen artist in front of them. They rapped along with it like it was part of the performance, but Luke's body was paralyzed by his agent's Medusa eyes. Termination.

Liquor.

The celebrity managed to utter the word, Money, and the spell broke. So he continued . . .

133

THE HIDDEN GENRE

(Luke Chase)

Money - Goals
Dope - Flows
Broke - Hoes?
Ain't Got - Those

Money - Goals
Watch Me - Pose
Fake - Bros?
Ain't Got - Those

The celebrity's "date" walked out on him. She abandoned him. Was she any different to Marge? Nah, unlike the latter, he knew exactly where Ruth was going. But that made it worse. Luke wasn't going to help her get there, that would be insult to injury. Instead, he put aggression into the next songs as if it was a punching bag.

It wasn't long before Isaac opened the front door of his house and found his crush, crushed.

THE FOLLOWING MORNING

THE HIDDEN GENRE

SIXTEEN

TAMMY OF North City News, Radio and Visuals had a live interview with the agent of the celebrity everyone was talking about, whether they were secular fans or not.

Isaac came into the lounge with two cups, but Ruth's attention was firmly on the TV screen. He put the cup down next to her before he took his seat on the other side.

"Thank you, Isaac," said Ruth.

"My pleasure . . ." he replied.

"I'm not just talking about the hot chocolate now," she looked him dead in the eyes like the night before, "thank you for everything, especially last night."

"I had a great time too," Isaac's shyness shied away, "I'm glad we've finally figured this thing out."

A shy smile tugged at her lips.

"Luke Chase gave a surprise performance last night," said Tammy to the audience, "as you can see on the video, he was performing, Money Goals, one of the songs that's on par with, So Enjoyable, for best song of the album, never mind single of the year. This morning, we got his agent, Nick Dobe, to talk on behalf of our favourite celebrity. Good morning, Nick."

"A very good morning indeed, Tammy," replied Nick, who sat opposite her, "let me just apologize to the audience first. I know how much they would rather listen to this month's Sexiest Man Alive, but right now he is currently having his beauty sleep, and that's why I'm here in his place."

"Oh, wow," said Ruth, not surprised, "this is going to be a long interview."

"Did everyone hear that? Sleep is very important for one to achieve success," said the host. "Tell me, Nick, what's Luke thinking?"

"That's an interesting question. I don't think I would be an agent if I could tell people what dreams you were having while you were sleeping, Tammy."

"*Very* long actually . . ." mumbled Isaac.

"I see what you did there, but I'm not referring to that. The people want to know why Luke Chase was performing in a church three days ago?" Tammy addressed the elephant in the room.

"Straight to the point, hey?"

"We have limited time to give our listeners and viewers the truth, agent Dobe."

"What was the question again?"

"Why was Luke performing in a church?"

"On Sunday?" stalled Nick.

"Yes . . ."

"Sunday's performance was nothing but him supporting his home town church. Rumor has it, he was asked to perform before the offering took place, and the church believes in the Holy Spirit guiding what the people give, which, if you ask me, is wrong, since I know from my time when I was going to church, it's nothing more or less than ten percent."

"Actually –" attempted Tammy.

"Anyway," continued Nick, "as I was saying, this took place before offering, and I'm not surprised that the Holy Spirit guided the people to give more than they ever had before. The Church, or the people in the building, whatever they call themselves these days, they should be thanking Luke Chase if anything."

Mrs. Banner walked into the lounge, "I can't believe the nerve of this agent . . ."

"I honestly don't know why Luke lets this guy speak on his behalf," said Isaac, "he is so good at lying and convincing at the same time, it's annoying . . ."

"I see," said Tammy, "but the problem is this: Luke was caught performing at a church one day and then a night club the next. After Sunday, people thought he could be another Saul-Paul type situation, but now they are starting to think he's just another wolf in sheep's clothing."

"I know it's Luke that the woman is targeting," said Mrs. Banner, "but I like the way she speaks with no fear or favor."

"I don't think you going to like the way the agent answers with no fear, mom," Isaac assured her.

"Let me first say this, so the public understands," said Nick, "Luke Chase is a Christian, or he is whatever they call it, if you rap and you a believer."

"A rapper that is Christian?" offered Tammy.

"Yes. He is a rapper that is Christian. He believes in God and all those good stuff. He will fall to his roots now and then, but it's nothing to worry about. His music won't change."

"I see. You know it was just last week when we had an interview with a secular artist who says a rapper that is Christian shouldn't exist. *'If Jesus told us to deny ourselves, why would you want people to know that you a rapper, before they know that you a follower?'* was his words. But let's ignore that for now and go with Luke Chase being a rapper that is Christian. There are still many out there that consider themselves such, but their material is completely different to Luke's."

"Yet I'm sure, as you know, the Bible has two parts? Have you read the Old Testament, and the things they did back then? Basically what you trying to say is, if Luke spoke about killing people to take land, you would have been fine with that?"

"That's a completely different discussion about the old and new covenant."

Nick Dobe chuckled in disbelief.

"However, what Luke wants to rap about is his choice, but when you say he is a rapper that is Christian, then he's got to stick to spreading the Gospel," said Tammy, "Luke Chase should just be known as a Hip Hop artist, because those rappers mention god whenever they feel like it, plus, the Bible says that you'll know a follower by their fruit, therefore -"

"I don't like how bias you sounding right now," said the agent.

"I'm telling you how it is, Agent Dobe. This is my job. If you going to speak about a topic, make sure you've studied it before throwing statements around. These things I have mentioned are the thoughts on the people's minds, regardless of the type of Hip Hop they listen to. And that's why Luke Chase performing two completely different type of songs caused such controversy."

"Look . . ." Nick Dobe took some time to reply, "Right now, Decep Records isn't paying him to perform songs from an album that we don't have copyrights to."

"I see," said Tammy. "If that's the reason to why your artist can't perform those songs, does that mean talks are ongoing to purchase the copyrights?"

"My client is currently touring his latest album, Tammy. Luke! Chase! Conquer! is what the fans are coming to see on Friday, and that's the theme they will be getting," insisted Nick.

"Then that's what -" Tammy was shown her cue by the producer, "it would appear we are out of time. Thank you for coming in to speak with us, Agent Dobe, it was great having you shed light on the situation." She turned to those in Mrs. Banner's lounge, "You heard it first here on North City News. Friday's concert will be going ahead as scheduled."

Promotions of Luke Chase's new album took to the screen.

"It's so obvious that they upset because Luke mentioned Jesus on a video that went viral," said Isaac, "and Tammy is right, the current contract he is under considers him a Hip Hop artist. Not a rapper that is Christian . . ."

Ruth stared at her cup with nothing to say.

"Okay, that's enough for the morning," Mrs. Banner clicked the TV off. "Do any of you have work today?"

"No -" tried Isaac.

"Yes, Mrs. Banner," replied Ruth.

Isaac got side eye from his mom.

"We both have a late shift," he corrected his answer, "Mrs. Rennells said she'll pick us up."

Isaac's mom looked at Ruth as if she needed confirmation.

"Isaac's telling the truth, Mrs. Banner," Ruth confirmed.

"Like really, mom?" Isaac shot a look at his mother.

"I'm just making sure," she walked to the kitchen with the empty cups, "normally people try to avoid work the morning after a concert. You know, call in sick . . ."

Isaac's phone shook.

"You had your phone on vibration?" asked Ruth, surprised considering that her colleague was waiting for a record label to get back to him, but more than anything, she was now curious to who it was.

"I didn't want any distractions," said Isaac as he grabbed his phone only to end up staring at it in disbelief.

"Who is it?" she put her thoughts to words.

"It's probably Chantal phoning to yell at you two for being late!" Mrs. Banner yelled from the kitchen.

Ruth checked her phone to be sure. No messages. She looked up and met Isaac's eyes.

"It's Luke . . ." he replied.

Ruth's stomach caved in. It was too soon to hear someone she knew mention *his* name.

Isaac on the other hand, had his mom's words replay in his head. Whether it was prophecy or not, it didn't matter. Luke was trying to organize a meet up just like she said he would.

"You should prepare yourself too, son."

"Prepare myself for what?" he had asked.

"For the day Luke comes knocking on that front door seeking advice."

Was this the exact time she spoke of?

SEVENTEEN

WOULD THE seven year contract really be worth it?

Isaac had a late shift and could only meet Luke after. What a crazy world the adults lived in. When they were younger, all they needed was one message and the boys would be on the court ready to ball. Nowadays, you needed to make an appointment to see people as if they were too busy running a business.

The sun stood there in the middle of the sky like the president giving a speech. The moon was in full attendance too. The words were warm and many embraced it in the cold world. However, when darkness came upon them, the sun would separate into an innumerable amount of lights to remind us to hold onto hope until its return.

Luke had many hours to kill before then, but no victims in mind.

"My Father," came a voice.

"Your father?" he asked, more out of confusion than anything.

The celebrity had, for a moment, forgotten where he was.

"You asked who I normally go to for advice," said the driver, "my Father is my go to guy."

"I don't know *my* father," confessed Luke.

"You wouldn't be in this situation if you did."

"What's that suppose to mean?"

"What about your mother, then?"

"Neither . . ."

"I'm sorry to hear that," sympathized the driver. "Does that mean you grew up in an orphanage?"

"The one and only North City Orphanage."

"Interesting, you say that, surely *there* is someone who cared for you."

"Yeah, but she abandoned me too . . ." added Luke.

"Sounds like you've had a hectic life."

"I don't think you understand how big of an understatement that is."

"It's probably as big as this city," agreed the driver, "but you're not the only one struggling and you can't keep driving around it. One day you need to stop, be grateful you alive, and then return to the reason why."

"Return to my . . . *purpose for living?*" Luke queried.

"Yes, but right now you've been driving around non-stop for twenty minutes. The bill's already high, but I'm willing to restart the meter, if you let me take you to the orphanage."

"I'm twenty, I can't go back to the orphanage," said the celebrity, but he couldn't fight the feeling that the uber driver meant it differently; just like Mrs. Rennells had, when she spoke about him impregnating her staff. "And why would you do something like that for me?" asked Luke.

"If it's true that you left the state three years ago, then you've missed the incredible development of the orphanage. I always thought the government was useless, but I guess they proved me wrong," said the driver, amazement in his voice, "plus, I need to go pick up my daughter."

+++

The car pulled up in front of the same old orphanage. So much for improvement. A regular kid got out of a regular Uber. Luke Chase was finally a regular person again. It was the label that made him so recognizable. Where would he be without them? He didn't know.

But the kids looking around, chasing each other and conquering ground, they would have recognized him had he not left.

When Luke made it through the front yard without one female drooling over him, he had to look back to be sure it actually happened.

What a bittersweet moment! Must be the outfit, since even Ruth recognized him in it. That's how common he appeared.

"Don't you love the view? Kids running around, playing around like they were family from the same parents," said a brunette staff member, "like -"

"Real brothers and sisters . . ." said the celebrity, because it was exactly what he considered Isaac and Ruth to be, but saying it out loud sounded . . . weird.

"Well well, if it isn't, Young Chaser?" said a familiar voice.

"Hi . . ." Luke turned to a different woman who approached them, "Ms. Miller, long time no see."

"Yes yes, I see now the type of person you've become," she said, "you haven't seen me in so many years, yet immediately you assume I'm lonely. I'm Mrs. Lonely. I haven't found *the one*. But I got news for you." Luke's face went pale before she concluded, "I'm very much happily single."

"Glad . . . to hear that . . . Ms. Miller?" he hesitated.

"That makes two of us." She turned to the staff member who had a grin on her face, "Thank you for all your hard work today, Gabi, please thank -"

The brunette's phone demanded attention. It was Kane. Gabi said her goodbyes to her senior and the random guy covered from head to toe.

It was cute. The guy dressed in the same outfit that Luke Chase had in the viral church video. Similar shades too. No idea how Mrs. Lonely recognized him though.

"What's up?" Gabi walked to the car, "I'm sorry, I can't join you tonight, Kane. I got to look after my little brother again. Yeah, my father's working a double shift tonight."

Kane? Was it *Margarette* Kane? Luke had been trying to find that woman ever since her little stunt at the church. Had she also said, a *double shift?* Guilt possessed his face as if he was the reason for the driver's struggles.

The celebrity had planned to withdraw a thousand stakes (Amborian Currency - ABS) as he only carried his card around. Yeah, Luke couldn't help them with cash right now, but he had to at least try something. More than anything, he had to try and get Margarette's number.

"What brings you home, Young Chaser?" Ms. Miller stopped him in his tracks, "Still chasing the ladies, I see."

"It's not like that . . ." he never thought those words would come out, at least, not having one hundred and ten percent truth to it, "There's a woman I'm looking for who goes by the name of Margarette Kane."

"Yes yes, she works here," said Ms. Miller casually, "that's her best friend, Gabi."

Luke turned around to chase after her but the car left as if the driver was taking his daughter as far away from the celebrity as possible.

"Don't worry, Young Chaser, I'll give you her number later. I'm anyway surprised you don't have it."

What was that suppose to mean?

"Come now, let's talk inside." Ms. Miller led the way, "I want to show you something."

+++

Ever since Luke left the orphanage, his growth had excelled. He gained meat on his bones, but the same couldn't be said about the hallways. He and Ms. Miller walked side by side conquering the space.

"That's everything I'm dealing with," said Luke, "right now, I don't know what to decide on."

"Yes yes, you got a huge choice to make at such a young age, but I'm not religious. You will have to speak to your friend from that angle."

Ms. Miller swore she heard Young Chaser's eyes hit the ground. What did he expect? It was like rushing someone to the doctor with the expectations for the person to be saved, regardless of the condition. Such high expectations that by the time you realize the doctor's only human and can't fix everything, you are too upset and crushed.

"However, I said I wanted to show you something, didn't I?" she put her hand on the door knob. It wasn't rusting, nor did it have cracks or chips. It was . . . new. So was the door. Ms. Miller opened them into a new world.

"A food court?" questioned Luke in awe.

"Yes yes, it's a food court," she said, proudly as if she designed it. "*This*, Luke, is just one of the improvements that your money has brought to the orphanage."

Luke was beyond speechless. His lips quivered from the lack of words. The joy radiating off the kids made his eyes watery. Hunger, was no longer a word in their dictionary.

"You've done more for us than the government," continued Ms. Miller, "yet people think it's them who has been aiding us. Those who don't trust the government to do something like this, they thought we were dealing drugs. We've even had police come here with a search warrant, all because of that rumor. Obviously they found nothing. I don't know what they were expecting."

"Ms. Miller, every month you thanked me for my contributions, it made me happy to know that my money was in good hands." Luke's voice was vulnerable, tears held on like a bungee jumper having second thoughts, "But actually seeing what the funds has done for the kids . . . I'm so glad to see them have what I never had. It's so enjoyable . . ."

"Don't cry on me just yet, Young Chaser," she said. "This is just the beginning."

+++

Ms. Miller showed the sponsor the bedrooms that they were currently working on. No more shall it be called bed chambers. It no longer felt like a prison. They had the warmth during winter that Luke never did.

Why had Marge abandoned him when the chance of seeing her everyday was why he endured the cold nights? He had lost his purpose for living back then. Pieces of his life were taken away, and unlike the moon, it didn't come back to complete him every month.

"Here we are," said Ms. Miller as they came upon another section. "Recognize it?"

"It's the sick bay," the celebrity answered with confidence.

"Yes yes, unfortunately you are correct."

"Because you were referring to the improvements, weren't you, Ms. Miller?"

They entered another corridor and Luke got sucked to the back room, "Well well, you sure remember your trauma room. Maybe your memory isn't as bad as you think."

"I don't think it's that . . . it's just . . . I could never forget something like that," struggled Luke, "to witness someone's head . . . everywhere . . . it was too much."

He couldn't stomach the memory. Ever since that day, he had been unable to remember names and memories of the past properly. Sometimes he couldn't even process the name of a person he met. It was as if *his* brain got blown apart and then put back incorrectly.

"Hey, Luke!" Ms. Miller brought him out of the past. "Let's get away from here and go have lunch together, shall we?"

+++

"Can I ask you a question, Ms. Miller?" Luke asked over lunch, "Do you know what happened to my parents?"

"You're wondering if I know anything about how you ended up at the orphanage?" Ms. Miller gave him a thorough look.

Was Luke ready to hear such?

"Okay," she decided he was, "only because I was there that night," the celebrity's heart stopped at her words. "It's only fair that I tell you what I know."

"You're saying you actually knew my parents and kept it from me all this time?" asked Luke, with a hint of anger.

"No, I said I'll tell you what I know about how you ended up here," she clarified, "I don't know who your parents are, Young Chaser, but there was a lot of child trafficking going on back then. The police brought you here when you were two years old. They said they found you in the house of a criminal they arrested. He was arrested for murder and drugs, not for child trafficking. The man said he didn't know who you were, but thought that the woman, who died that day, probably stole you . . ."

"Stole me? Was she going . . .?" it all clicked for the celebrity. "She was going to sell me . . .?" *Liquor.*

Ms. Miller nodded to Luke's statement, it was better than admitting the terrible reality of what could have happened to him. How one night changed the course of his life.

"I can't believe this," continued the celebrity. "This is the reason why my parents haven't tried contacting me . . . they think I'm dead?" *Liquor.*

Ms. Miller had eighteen years to play the night over and over in her head, it didn't make sense. She checked the missing children reports. Luke's face and name wasn't even a rumor to them. She had contacted the NCPA regarding the issue, but a Detective Rennells ensured her not to let it steal her sleep. The kid would be informed when he was old enough to understand. Ms. Miller's sleep returned after hearing how sincere the woman was.

"Don't let it get you down, Young Chaser," she finally said, "look at how you turned out. You've grown into a respectful and handsome young man. Not everyone gives back the way you do. Your desire to not have it public shows your humility. You have a good heart, Luke."

Did he really? Everything he did for the orphanage was because he had a chance to make something of his life and he grabbed it with both hands. He would've been kicked out at eighteen, at least according to the rules, had he not won the competition. None of these improvements would be possible if it wasn't for Decep Records.

"Whatever decision you make," continued Ms. Miller, "just know, we will always be grateful for what you've done."

If this much good came from the last three years, how much more would come from an extra seven? Would the seven year contract really be worth it? The answer was a no-brainer, yet Isaac's opinion he still longed for.

And what a night it would turn out to be.

EIGHTEEN

ISAAC PULLED up to the beach bar. He put the car to sleep, rolled down the window, and laid back to stare at the stars that applied social distancing. The waves were violent, unlike how he wanted the night to go. Especially since Luke wouldn't have asked to meet him if it wasn't serious.

The celebrity's decision to move East, where Decep Records' HQ was, was a decision he made on his own. He knew what he wanted and ran straight for it. No advice needed. Therefore, him asking to meet Isaac showed his indecisiveness.

"Adon," said Isaac, eyes up, "please give me the words to say tonight."

"Get out the car, dude," said a man, who sat on the bonnet of his jeep with a girl by his side, "the view's much better out here."

With a shy smile, Isaac took the guy's advice and got a raised glass for his bravery.

The entrance to the bar was inviting as the doors received him with open arms. Upon entry he was hit by the stench of liquor, while the speakers threw out a relaxed vibe.

Luke was at the counter with his head in his hands and fingers digging into his skull. Isaac took a breath, one deep breath to calm himself down like he was taught at North High. The celebrity switched position in a split second. He now sipped his drink, but in the same rhythm as the music. A few more blinks was necessary to confirm what had actually occurred.

Maybe this would be easier than Isaac's mind made it out to be.

"Hold on, pretty boy," a buff woman appeared out of thin air, "I need to see some ID."

"ID?" Isaac mimicked as the words struggled for definition in his brain. "Oh, identification . . . here we go."

"22, hey?" she gave him a thorough glance. "You too young for me, move along."

Isaac froze at the rejection, or was it confusion? The woman moved on before he could come to a conclusion.

"If I didn't know better," said Isaac to Luke, after the paralysis wore off, "I would think you've been here in that same outfit drinking since Sunday."

He got no response. It may be worse than Isaac originally thought.

"Can I get you something to drink, sir?" asked the bartender. "A beer, cider, juice, anything but –"

"Water will be fine please," said Isaac, innocently.

He took his seat next to Luke after he got a dirty look from the bartender, who was meant to make him feel welcomed. So much for customer service.

"What's his problem?" Isaac asked Luke.

"He can't understand why we come to a bar if we just going to drink water," came the reply.

"Thank you," Isaac got his glass. He turned to the celebrity, "Are you hinting to that being water in yours?"

"I need a sober mind to make the right decision," said Luke, "liquor does the exact opposite. So I rather not risk it . . ."

A wave of relief came upon Isaac. Sober minded Luke would listen to reason. He did so whenever Mr. Banner spoke. Surely the son was no different, "Why am I here Luke? What did you want to speak about?"

"Ruth?"

Was that it? Did Luke invite him, all the way to a place he hadn't been before, just to ask about Ruth? Did she tell him about their potential relationship?

"She's fine," Isaac finally said, "just disappointed about how the evening went."

"Yeah . . . I'm between a rock and a hard place, bro," admitted Luke, "I wanted advice, so I needed to know if you are the friend you claim to be."

"That explains why you invited me to a bar, considering – "

"I needed to see if you'd show up regardless," he took a sip of his water, "and I'm grateful to have you here. I honestly don't know how to go about the situation . . . sunday's service didn't exactly help anything."

"Why? Is this about Margarette?" asked Isaac, wondering what the deal was with her.

"Nah, it ain't," a smile appeared on the celebrity's face, "but I finally got her number though."

"How?"

"She works at the orphanage, but this isn't about her," said Luke, the smile fading as quick as it appeared, "it's about me and the seven year contract. It has nearly been a week since I told you about it; what are your thoughts?"

"Take the contract and spread the Word," said Isaac, with no hesitation.

"It doesn't work like that, bro."

"Then I believe you should repent, come back to the Father and finally get baptized," added Isaac.

"How will that help me though?" asked the celebrity.

"The Holy Spirit will have a good influence on your decisions, bro."

"But I believe Jesus died and rose, Isaac. That doesn't change the fact that I keep choosing the option that benefits my career, over and over again," said Luke. "Why do I do it, bro? Why am I willing to listen to the Word, but can't stick to it?"

"Bro!" there it was. The reason why Mrs. Banner was led to the parables. Word of mouth. From parent to son. From son to friend. "Can I read you something quick?" Isaac pulled out his phone after Luke gave the go ahead, "God is great! It always amazes me the way

He makes all things work together for our good. My mom was actually reading a parable that may have your answer. Okay, here it is. Matthew thirteen."

Luke chuckled. He couldn't believe it. Out of all the sixty six books, the one book he read that night was Matthew. Was now a good time to admit he skipped the parables due to a lack of understanding?

"'Behold, a sower went to sow. And as he sowed, some seed fell by the wayside; and the birds came and devoured them. Some fell on stony places, where they did not have much earth; and they immediately sprang up because they had no depth of earth. But when the sun was up they were scorched, and because they had no root they withered away. And some fell among thorns, and the thorns sprang up and chocked them. But others fell on good ground and yielded a crop: some a hundredfold, some sixty, some thirty. He who has ears to hear, let him hear.'"

"I have ears and I heard every word," said Luke, "yet I still don't understand what is being said."

"Me too . . ." said the bartender.

"When did you join this?" the celebrity asked the eavesdropper.

"Oh, last week," he replied, aware of what was asked, "the bartender that worked here got arrested for trying to kill some lame celebrity."

Was he referring to the incident at the Grand Fortuna? Couldn't be . . . that guy wasn't trying to kill him, plus, this bartender called the celebrity *lame*. A title *Luke Chase* was far from.

Isaac put his phone away and finished his water. The bartender refilled the glass immediately like buying more data so Isaac would stop buffering.

"The water's on the house if you explain," he said.

"There's four types of people who hear the Word," Isaac explained. "What was the first one?"

They stared at him as if he was an exam paper: one they hadn't studied for.

"It's the one who received the seed by the wayside," he continued, "this is for anyone who hears the Word and does not understand it, then the devil comes and takes it away from their hearts."

"That sounds like me," confessed the bartender, "but it may not be. I don't know. It depends. Does the stony places got anything to do with smoking weed?"

"No, they are people who hear the Word and immediately receive it with joy, but they have no root in themselves, so they only endure for a while; for when tribulation or persecution arises because of the Word, immediately they stumble."

"Bro . . ." mumbled the celebrity, disappointed, "I think that could be me."

"I don't think that's you, bro."

Luke's eyes flickered with hope.

"You are currently worse than that," added Isaac.

Luke's heart stopped like the current song in the bar. The next beat began soon after.

"Yo, bruh!" yelled a man from a group of people. "Can we like get a drink over here?"

"Please, excuse me," the bartender went to help the new customers.

Luke stared at his glass of water as if he was asking himself the question: half empty or half full?

The bartender returned with a smile, "Is our lame celebrity the thorn then?"

"What did you say?" Luke glared at the bartender in a way that one couldn't tell if it was because he was called the thorn, or because he was called lame.

"Jesus explained this to the disciples," Isaac said quickly and carefully, "he who received seed among the thorns is he who hears the Word, but the cares of this world and the deceitfulness of riches choke the Word, and he becomes unfruitful."

"Yeah," a cold breeze came over Luke's body, "that . . . that explains it . . ."

"I don't think you need to explain the last one. I get it now," said the bartender, "please enjoy the water."

"Wait, wasn't the water free to begin with?" asked Isaac, aware of the answer.

The bartender left his shift grinning.

"Thank you, bro. Thank you for being honest with me. I finally understand my situation now," said Luke, "you know, I was just as surprised as you when I won that competition three years back, but I believed it to be God putting me on my path of destiny. After that, everything happened so fast. My dream to be a rapper was nothing but hopeful thinking. Me being optimistic as you know. But then and there in black and white, it could become a reality. All they needed was a signature."

"You got caught in the moment?" asked Isaac.

"They told me they would have signed me regardless if I won or not. They had the smiles on their faces that I only saw when the pastor invited people to the alter. It seemed so genuine. They saw the potential in me. They believed in my talent. They showed me real love. But now . . ."

Luke continued to stare at the water as if he was waiting for it to reveal the answer.

"But now?" Isaac pushed.

"I thought *I* was really into money. But Nick's next level money hungry. I see it now; he only really listened to me whenever it came to making money. I tried to talk to God again, because He listens. Problem is, all He does is listen. I never got a response and then people got the nerve to tell me to repent and seek the Kingdom first."

"You know God speaks through His people."

"What? You're also going to say that He's using you to speak to me right now?"

"Maybe He is," said Isaac. "I mean you got the answer to your question, didn't you?"

Luke's lips sealed closed and his eyes fell onto the water again. Half full or half empty?

"Come on, bro." Isaac stood up, "Let me show you something."

NINETEEN

ISAAC DRAGGED his best friend to the courts. They weren't on trial, but had come here before for trials. However, that got cancelled when the rain washed the day away. The light posts had a new design to them, they focused on certain spots while the darkness snaked around them. One, close to an occupied court, was flickering as if it was nervous.

"Why would you bring me here of all places?" asked Luke. "This is where . . . bro . . . we witnessed *it* . . ."

"I know," Isaac sat on the small patch of grass relaxing on a hill, "but I overcame it . . . it's now your turn."

"Is that why you brought me here?" Luke glared at the small crowd, "not for some early traumatic surprise party?"

"I almost forgot!" said Isaac, faking excitement, "today's your birthday, bro!"

"Yeah," Luke sat down, not biting, "very funny."

Back then, a man had walked as if he was on a mission in the courts. And he had been. He had to carry out an assassination. Basketball games were everywhere, but only one game got physical; Luke vividly expressed that the opponents were cheating. He was called a girl and shirts were torn when they pulled each other closer, their lips moved with passion, but it was in no way romantic. The opponent had told him to do something and see what would happen, but the man on a mission walked up to his target in Luke's arms, put the gun to his head and pulled the trigger.

"I know your birthday's on Sunday," said Isaac. "That's why you wanted to have a final concert here, right?"

The deafening memory echoed in Luke's ear preventing a reply, or was it because he didn't want to admit such a sensitive truth?

"They say, when you think about quitting, remember why you started," added Isaac.

"What's that got to do with anything?" Luke asked.

"In your case," came the reply, "I want you to think about why you wanted to make it so badly."

"Why I wanted to make it?" the celebrity thought out loud. "To get out of the orphanage and these streets as soon as possible. Marge abandoned me. I wanted to go to a public school where I could meet someone with the same goals in mind as me."

"Bro . . . did you use me as a rebound?" asked Isaac, sarcastically.

"You know I don't sway that way," said Luke, "I needed a friend I could trust. Marge at least taught me how to protect myself, but it got me in trouble more than anything."

"That's what you get for going around punching people for no reason."

"Ms. Miller told me to stand up to my bullies though."

"Not knock them out," replied Isaac, "that's completely different."

"Yeah," chuckled Luke. "So basketball became a blessing, not a distraction? Is that what you trying to say?"

"Not exactly, but we can go with that. Remember, we may have been in the same school, but this is where we actually met. On the courts."

"Cause you, being as small as you are, can actually play ball," Luke admitted, "that's why."

"Didn't stop you from beating me every time though."

"Didn't stop you from keeping me on my toes, bro."

"Funny you say that when you blessed with that above average height."

"Thing is, you up to par with me in basketball," said Luke, "but here I am still wishing I'm half as good as you when it comes to music."

"Says the famous rapper," joked Isaac, "you want to settle this in a one on one boxing match?"

They laughed, and moments after, a few girls broke away from the crowd in the occupied court.

"Ruth . . ." mumbled the celebrity.

"Bro?"

"This is where we saw Ruth for the first time," said Luke, "she was walking with her friends."

Both had stared at the group of girls for too long back then. Luke had shifted his eyes the moment one of Ruth's friends took the stare as an invitation.

He always had eyes for Ruth, but was it only a reaction to Marge's absence? Luke never got romantic with her; however, he was eleven and Marge was fourteen when she left the orphanage. Had he ever thought about her in such a way? All this time, was Ruth *just* a rebound?

Nah, it couldn't be. He considered Ruth for marriage once. No one considered a rebound for marriage. But the way she looked at Isaac, and vice versa, as if they wanted each other; it irritated him.

There was a time when Luke felt like the one who married Ruth would be declared the victor between the two of them. But was that *just* the heat of competition? Did he really like Ruth for her, or to have one over Marge and Isaac? He didn't know anymore.

"I brought you here for one reason," said Isaac, "and that was to remind you of why you chased your dream –"

"I know –"

"Not to remind me of the day I fell in love," he finished with a mumbled.

The crowd went crazy as if the words echoed throughout the courts. Isaac finally admitted it to himself. Luke heard it as well. It was soft, but he heard it.

"It's a battle," Isaac stood. "Let's go check it out."

+++

A man was at the center of the attention. People were patting him and shaking his hand like he just saved the world.

"No idea who he is," said Isaac.

"That's Cash Money," said Luke, "I met him at a concert organized by Nick."

"Why am I not surprised?"

Another man calmed the crowd down to give the opponent an opportunity to respond. "Let's welcome, Mkay."

The artist stepped forward to face her opponent.

"Margarette?" the two friends said in union.

The beat boxer's sound had strong bass with a hint of dubstep.

(Mkay)

You like to call out the haters
They all want what you deserve?
You like to call out the fakers
Their jealously gets on your nerves?
But the wages of sin be death
Punishment would only have one left
He lived His life perfect and suffered crucifixion
Through such He has brought us redemption
Yes, I confess that Jesus Christ is my Saviour
How do you know this? Just check my behaviour
You go see those fruits in full blossom
So no mourning if I'm put in a coffin
Cause He said I'll rise from the dark
And yes, the fire in me started with a spark
I was lost, walking with my eyes closed
Now I'm found, talking till my eyes close

No one spoke. The first four lines were digested by the crowd, its build up was legendary. But then she started preaching. He raised questions; she answered. Not one bar really called Cash Money out or dissed him, complete opposite to the opposition. Accordingly to the streets and the streets alone, it was a disappointing response.

"And the winner is," the judge avoided Mkay's glare, "Cash Money."

The people reacted out of sheer relief more than shock. The judge needed to make a decision so the loser could leave and they could go on to the next battle. But Margarette's night was still young.

"Is that how it is?" she asked, "I lost the battle because I never glorified murder? I never glorified drugs. I never glorified sin in general, and so I lost?"

"Let it go, Mkay," said the judge.

"No! That rap had more deeper meaning than his life!"

"Oh, snap," commented someone amongst the murmurs.

"This is not the time, Margarette," Isaac sided with the judge.

"Isaac? How long have you been here?"

"Long enough . . ."

Luke stayed out of it, but he had a full view of proceedings.

Cash Money was shaking with agitation. He had won the battle, yet all the attention was on the loser and some random spectator. He unzipped his jacket to get some of that cool breeze drifting among them. Luke's nerves sky rocketed. The winner of the battle was loaded. And it had nothing to do with cash/money. In fact, the revealed handle was like the ones the officers had.

"This is why it's really risky to battle in the streets with the streets being the judge," said Isaac, "it's like getting out of the boat thinking you can walk on water."

"I don't know, Isaac," said Luke, "Peter walked just fine when he had his eyes on Jesus."

The celebrity did the exact thing he ought not to. He drew attention. All of it was on Luke, the moment the little knowledge he gained from reading Matthew, slipped out. He was recognized immediately as phones were whipped out to take pictures and videos without his permission. Cash Money wasn't going to let this slip. You want to know the perfect opportunity to become famous? Defeat Luke Chase in a street battle.

TWENTY

THE LIGHT post flickered with more frequency as if it tried to mimic everyone's panicked hearts. Were they about to witness an internationally known local artist get schooled in his backyard, or would the celebrity increase the fame in his reputation? It sure was a mountain to climb. Recently, Luke was known for music, not battles. This was a completely different ball game. But the streets never cared for excuses from the victims in its path.

"What's it gonna be, Chase?" asked Cash Money.

"Don't you see it? I'm famous, you're not a threat," said Luke, "time is money, so spending it on you will just put me in debt."

"Oh, snap," the words jumped out amongst the laughs.

Cash Money looked around and licked his lips as if he needed someone to sponsor him with something to eat, never mind a deal. He had the spotlight like he wanted, so why couldn't he think of a reply? It wasn't his style to delay. Everyone waited, but his hand twitched to grab the strap rather.

"I think you're scared of me," he finally said, "last time I checked, I released my album on time, unlike *you*."

The crowd was hostile with their reactions, there were no friends here. All eyes turned to Luke, they wanted him to wipe that smug off his opponent's face. But at the same time, they wanted Cash Money to respond afterward like nothing happened. This crowd wasn't loyal to anyone anymore, all they really wanted was entertainment.

The celebrity chuckled. If that's what they wanted. That's what he would give them. Luke knew how to entertain people; he did it for a living. However, his friends were worried to how he would go about this entertainment. The streets were short tempered and not very forgiving.

Like a real hater, Cash Money brought up the past, but he wasn't lying. Luke's album *was* late and Decep Records refused to give a reason to the public. The artist's career was believed to have ended before it started. An anticipated failure.

But then Luke! Chase! Conquer! happened. It sky rocketed all types of rating to a point that it was believed, if the album wasn't so successful, the label would have crashed had they given no explanation, to the fans, to why the album was delayed.

Luke intensified his glare at the opponent who self proclaimed victory. He walked towards Cash Money with purpose and the crowd made way for him as if he was royalty. Then again, compared to them, he was. They were being disrespectful when they should have been honoured to be in his presence.

"Don't do this, bro," said Isaac.

"He's not worth it," tried Margarette.

"You are correct, he isn't," said the celebrity, "but I need to make sure *he* knows that."

Luke halted. Cash Money's smug faltered. The celebrity was up to something. He searched his pockets as if he lost something. But the opponent was having none of it. He steadily reached towards his belt. Finally it was found.

"Congratulations, Cash Money," Luke whipped out a few hundred stakes he drew earlier, before the bar visit, and put it in his opponent's pocket, "considering that your album didn't do much for you financially, I was seriously voting for you to lose against Mkay. Guess you proved me wrong, Payton."

161

"My man!" reacted a spectator, "your street name reached the big stage, dawg."

"Street name?" chuckled Luke. "According to my agent, Payton Rogers' stage name is Cash Money."

"Hold up," said the judge. "You saying that Payton is actually this chump's *real* name?"

"Yeah," replied Luke. "What? Did you guys think it was his nickname or something?"

"We did, as a matter of fact." The judge faced the man in question, "Dawg, you said that you killed a Ryvil and got *paid a ton* for it. That's how you got the street name, Payton."

Had Luke exposed something he knew nothing about?

"That's how it went down!" replied Cash Money, "real talk! All facts! Don't listen to him, dawg!"

"You know, I would have taken your word for it if I hadn't seen the bank statements you've been trying to hide," added the judge.

"That doesn't matter right now!" insisted Payton, "it has nothing to do with the battle! Can't you see what he's doing? He tryna get out this battle. Chase is scared to lose to me cause he knows it will destroy his reputation!"

"Not true," said Luke. "But that does make me wonder if that's the reason you don't use *your* real name?"

"Oh, snap . . ."

The battle was over before it began. Luke ignored every word *Broke Beggar* spat out afterwards. Payton faced the back of Luke Chase like he did in the industry, nothing new. The chance to make a name for himself slowly slipped from his grasp with every step the celebrity took. The videos would most likely go viral. His career would most likely end. His life would most likely return to the one he escaped. He couldn't let it happen. He couldn't go back. He had to try something. Anything. If the person wouldn't budge, maybe someone close would.

"Last time I checked, you don't use your real name either."

Margarette and Isaac stopped dead in their tracks. Mkay and Yahshuandi, the Gospel Rapper, were their stage names, no different to Cash Money. But who was Payton targeting?

"Yahshuandi, or you can call me the Gospel Rapper," he mocked. "Why you so quiet, huh?"

Isaac gave the demon side eye.

"We heading to the crib, Payton," said the judge, "you already got some explaining to do. Don't make it worse."

"No!" he would not go back to that life.

(Cash Money)

All he does is talk - he got no raps
Yet you see my walk - stacks on stacks
So much paper, I could make a newsroom
And I don't feel like reporting about the Groom
Telling us that the Church is Jesus' bride
Showing us that Church is not a building
I'm starting to think that it all involved a bribe
I refuse to believe in Him ever rising

If the tension wasn't there before, it sure was now. Isaac was half way before Luke and Margarette caught up to him.

"Bro, what are you doing? You cannot challenge him."

"You yourself said battling in the streets is not a good idea."

Isaac stopped, "Luke himself already debunked that statement, Margarette."

"I did?"

"Look, I'm not challenging him, and I'm not battling him either," said Isaac, "I'm simply going to do what Jesus did to the Pharisees."

"Correction?" mumbled Margarette, "I understand. But be careful, Isaac. Remember what happened in the temple. This is still the courts . . ."

"Plus, they don't point it out, they just point and pull triggers." Joe's words echoed in her mind.

Luke wasn't so willing as her. This could quickly get out of hand. The enemy had a gun and was jumpy. Who knew what defeat would trigger? Plus . . . the celebrity had already witnessed someone's head blown apart before. No way did he want the same done to his *best* friend.

The Gospel Rapper wasn't going to walk away from this though, he had a one track mind. His Saviour had been disrespected with false accusations. He wasn't going to let it slide. Yes, Payton visibly had a weapon, but God was on the side of His people, who did Isaac have to fear?

Luke gave in and let him go to war.

Isaac marched straight to Payton with such confidence, it was intimidating. Every step closer and closer as if he didn't fear death. The latter stepped slightly back as a defense mechanism, but it was futile.

(Yahshuandi, the Gospel Rapper)

Whether you believe now
Or reject to chase nothing but success
On that great day every knee shall bow
And every tongue shall confess
That Yahshua is Adon
The One who reigns - heaven's only entry
The Father's only begotten Son
Everything else we chase is just vanity

Everyone was still as the breeze tickled the fences. Meanwhile, each line that was spoken got dissected. They understood everything that was said as if they were daily readers in the Word. No one knew why and how it was possible. But they all knew that Payton had lost the battle. He couldn't respond with words to that.

Eyes flew the rapper's way for a response, but reality hit him too. He twitched for the strap again. It was his go to right now. If not words, maybe actions would do justice. So what if he didn't kill a Ryvil? He would show that it didn't mean he couldn't kill a human.

"You know what?" Payton's hand slowly slithered towards his belt, "you love your Jesus so much, huh? Why don't you die for him motha -"

A gunshot cut through the words and flesh of a human.

TWENTY-ONE

JOE WARNED her about this, but not once did Margarette think she would see it play out. Her life flashed before her eyes as quick as the shot echoed throughout the courts. The scream was terrifying as a body beside her hit the floor as if it was dropped from the sky. She managed to take a glance. It was a teenager that got hit in the abdomen. Blood raced towards the tar beneath him as he moaned uncomfortably. Almost everyone ran for their lives as if he was a ticking time bomb. And he was. But he wasn't going to explode. He was going to die.

This thought never crossed the minds of those who were taught to look out for themselves. The streets was all about the survival of the fittest. Margarette herself prepared to flee the moment Joe's warning took hold of her thoughts. So when push came to shove, she fled.

The gun shot gave the light post such a fright that it went out as if it fled as well. Payton had every intention to give Isaac a headshot, but ended up getting one instead. His body fell stiff on the ground with potential to become cold and non-living like the weapon that skidded on the floor.

The gun had nearly made it to the Gospel Rapper's face before Luke got involved. Isaac looked death in the eyes, but surprising, he saw no one. No one came to his mind. Not even Ruth, never mind his mom. No thoughts of joining his father either. Did it all happen too quick for his brain to process the possibility, or did he really not fear death?

"Thank you, Father," Isaac mumbled as a tear involuntarily rolled down his cheek.

Luke had slowly sneaked up to Payton during the silence. The situation was too tense for anyone to hold off the temptation of wiping out their enemy right there and then. The gun, Cash Money had on him, made it enviable. One didn't have to live in the streets to see that it was only a matter of time before Payton turned to it for answers. There was no way the celebrity was willing to witness the death of someone close to him. Even abandoning him like what happened at the orphanage was better than permanently leaving, as much as Luke was wrong about Marge doing so back then. She had abandoned him without his knowledge this evening. But her reactions would prove to do more good than harm.

The lights from the other posts got brighter as if they were working harder to try and help in anyway possible. Soon the humans could see through the darkness around them. Isaac and Luke were the only ones left. They stood over a teen with a bullet in him, and an adult who showed no signs of getting up anytime soon. Both had nothing in common but a lack of a possible future. A pond of blood slowly formed around the kid.

"He's losing a lot of blood," said Isaac.

Luke couldn't stand the sight. The teen was much better off, he had a bullet in his stomach, but it just sat there. The butterflies in Luke's stomach became pacmen and began eating him from the inside out. He tried to control his breathing like Isaac, like he was taught at North High, but witnessing someone get shot again brought back memories he didn't want to remember. The celebrity left the state, travelled the world, filled his brain with the beauty that it had to offer, yet one spark of the past formed an uncontrollable blaze of it. He crouched down to try and corner the pacmen into dead ends, but it didn't help much.

Isaac's body slowly adapted to the situation as he took control of his breathing. He calmly focused on the two bodies he had in front of him.

Should he put pressure on the kid's wound, or check if the man was still breathing?

The kid moaned as if instructing he was alive and needed help more urgently.

"Maybe you really *should* become a boxer," said Isaac as he put pressure on the wound, "you knocked him clean out."

Luke chuckled, "Now's not the time for jokes, bro."

"And what about a *thanks*?"

"There is never not a time for that," he replied, grinning, "thank you."

"I should be thanking you for saving my life," said Isaac, "not the other way around."

"You would have done the same for me," Luke's body calmed down as he took his mind off things, "that's what best friends do, they look out for each other." He stood up and turned a blind eye to the situation, "It was no different to what Peter did."

"Except, Payton still has his ear on his head," said Isaac, curious to Luke's sudden use of references to Peter, "bro, please phone the ambulance."

"Yeah, I'm on it . . ." Luke searched himself, "Bro, either I got pick pocketed, or I left my phone in the car?"

"Come on," the decision Isaac made hit him flat in the face. "Why tonight out of all nights?"

"We left it in the car, right?"

"Yes, I wanted us to stay focused on the reason we came here tonight, remember?" It didn't matter whether Luke remembered it or not. What mattered was what he did next. "Bro, you need to go to the car and fetch the phone."

"Okay –"

"But first check if Payton's still breathing –"

"No . . ."

Surely Isaac's brain was playing games with him, "Bro, did you just say, *no*?"

"Sounds like you heard me."

Maybe some other day Isaac would have been impressed with Luke's usage of *no* instead of *nah*, but this wasn't the time or place to be practicing English. "Are you being serious right now?" he asked.

"Why don't you do it?" replied the celebrity.

"He's too far from me for me to do both, Luke."

"What if he's dead, Isaac? I will not have my finger prints on his body."

"Come on! You can't be serious? Now is not the time to think about yourself!"

"Have you already forgotten that he tried to kill you?" Luke made the mistake of turning around.

"Don't –"

It was too late. The celebrity's mind was gone and he began walking up and down as a failed defense mechanism. "This is why I don't rap about the gangster life. Killing people like it's nothing ain't nothing. It's too much. How does one even do such? All for the sake of money and respect? Would I kill for money? Nah, it's too much. For respect? Oh, respect . . . Payton must have a lot of friends who respect him. They're going to come for me. They will want revenge after the funeral. My life's over."

"Bro! Come on! Snap out of it!"

"They will *pay a ton* for me to be assassinated." Luke scared himself with laughter, "Goodbye brains . . ."

Isaac was beyond irritated. He needed to ensure his best friend that Payton was alive and well. Maybe not well, but alive. Luke would have to shut up, calm down and go phone the ambulance then. But to do that, Isaac had to let go and trust that the kid wouldn't slip away. He lessened the pressure slowly. Slowly the pressure was lessened like teaching someone to drive for the first time. He let go completely.

"It . . . burns . . ." the kid managed to utter out, desperately, "Hel . . . help . . ."

Isaac's legs moved quicker than he rapped. Payton's jacket was thankfully already zipped opened. He planted his ear against Payton's chest. Nothing. There was nothing. When did Luke become a rival for One Punch Man? No. There it was. A heartbeat.

Faint. But it was there. It was like the little knowledge Payton had on Jesus was keeping him alive.

"Bro! He's alive!"

Luke hadn't escaped the maze yet.

"Come on." Isaac ran to put pressure on the kid's wound, "Payton's alive! I need you to phone the ambulance!"

Still no response. Maybe if he threw Luke with the keys.

"No . . ." whispered the celebrity, who made it out of the maze with the sirens as a guide, "it's the cops."

"Finally –"

"No, this is bad, Isaac."

"This is good! Not bad!" Isaac was tipping over the edge, "I'm stressed out here literally holding a life in my hands while you struggling to hold yours together."

"You don't get it, bro," said Luke, "I can't go to prison –"

"He's alive, Luke! Payton is alive! You're not going to prison!"

Hope formed in Luke's eyes, but disappeared the moment he looked at the man on the floor, "It doesn't look like he's breathing though."

"Go put your ear on his chest and hear for yourself."

"I'm not going to touch him, Isaac. We need to leave or else we will be locked up!"

"I'm not like you," said Isaac, "I will not abandon this kid, Luke."

"What's that suppose to mean? You know what? I don't want to know," he replied, "we wouldn't have been in this situation had you walked away like I did. Nah, you had to be right. You had to prove that you can out rap someone who belongs to a secular label."

Was that really the reason? Did Isaac's mind subconsciously get him involved in something he could have avoided, in the name of defeating a professional artist? No. That wasn't the reason. Payton made statements and he confronted them. That's what happened.

"I'm leaving . . ." Luke walked away, "You will have to deal with the consequences of this on your own. My label won't be able to help *me*, never mind you."

"You really believe that?" Isaac asked mockingly.

"Yeah, I do," Luke gave Isaac side eye, "Decep Records doesn't get themselves involved with bribery."

"I don't know, Luke," said Isaac, "they seemed fine bribing the judges three years ago."

TWENTY- TWO

IT WAS the season of early nights for the sun, which had no energy to stay up late. Margarette had no energy to continue, but she pushed. It was a case of running until you felt dead, rather than being dead. It didn't help that she ran in the opposite direction of her car. Why was she still running? *How* was she still running? Was it safe to stop? Her body gave in as she tried to catch her breath, and the wave of fatigue came over her while her lungs raged with fire. She found shelter, but even the water was useless against the burn in her chest. The bottle was gulped down as if she escaped the desert in desperate need of water.

"Do you have a phone on you?" she asked. "I need to phone an ambulance."

"Are you going to pay for that water?" asked the cashier.

"I don't have money on me."

"Maybe you should have thought of that before you drank it. I'm phoning the police instead."

"No, phone emergency services," said Margarette, "there's a kid shot in the courts."

The cashier's fingers froze. "My kid went to the courts," he mumbled.

"Kid? Uhm, boy or girl?" Margarette slowly took the phone from him, "The kid who got shot sounded like a girl, but the body was heavy when it hit the ground. So it could have been a boy."

"Please, don't say that . . ."

"Papa!" a boy ran into the shop with tears flowing down his cheeks, "I love you, papa!"

The cashier embraced the kid while the phone rang and rang as if it searched desperately for a signal that it could latch onto. It caught one.

"Yes, hello!"

"What's your emergency?" asked a voice, super relaxed.

"Someone's been shot at the courts!" yelled Margarette.

"Where are you, mam?"

"Did you not hear me? I said a kid got shot in the *courts*!"

"Please calm down, mam."

"Don't tell me to calm down!"

"Please tell me where are you, mam?"

"North City! Where else?"

"Where in North City? Are you by the *High Courts*, mam?"

"No –"

"Where are you, mam?"

"Where am I?" she looked at the cashier, "I'm . . ."

"Sable way," he said.

"I'm in Sable way."

"So you referring to the basketball courts, mam?"

"Yes!"

"Okay," said the voice before the clicking of buttons filled the silence. "Yes, the NCPA have been alerted and are on their way already. We'll be sending an ambulance immediately. Thank you for your assistance, citizen. Stay indoors and may you have a great evening."

The breeze picked up like the anticipation before an anime fight. Luke faced off against Isaac with the latter having his hands down in a summoning jutsu attempt. The former gave his opponent a taste of his own medicine: side eye.

The moaning stopped as if the kid wanted to hear the end of this before his end. Silence. Whether Payton was dead or not was irrelevant compared to the statement made by Luke's best friend. He could maybe let it go if it was a critic, but it was not. The accusation was coming from the one he defeated fair and square. Something a sore loser would claim. Something no one expected from Isaac.

"Is that suppose to be some kind of joke?" asked Luke. "Cause it ain't funny."

"No . . ." replied Isaac, "it's not a joke, bro . . ."

What was wrong with him? The bribery was a light truth as long as Isaac kept it in the dark. Then he went and slipped up. Now the weight threatened to crush him, and those involved.

"I meant to say, *cops*," he lied, "you yourself said that Nick bribed the cops in America."

"Nah, I heard you clearly." Luke turned completely, "I didn't think it was true, but you really are jealous of me. Why else would you make such a wild accusation?"

"Now's not the time for this," said Isaac, "we got more important things at hand."

"Yeah, like leaving this place before the cops shoot us!"

"I'm not leaving this kid, Luke! How can you leave someone behind so easily?"

"I wouldn't leave if he was related to me and he isn't . . . he's just a random kid in the wrong place at the wrong time, so yeah, I'm leaving."

The kid's consciousness slipped more and more as blood slipped out of his body more and more. It wasn't long before he was on the edge and slipped into a coma. Isaac's attempts to help was futile. The kid wasn't dead, at least not yet. But he would be soon. And all Isaac could do was wait and watch as Luke got further and further away. He couldn't hold it in anymore.

"Why did you leave Ruth?" he asked.

Luke froze, "What's that suppose to mean?"

"I think you know exactly what I mean."

"All this time," the celebrity turned to face the Gospel Rapper. "You knew about us?"

"She recently told me what you did to her, Luke."

"My career was more important, okay."

"How can your career be more important than your –"

"What if we broke up? What then? Huh? Then the sacrifice would have been in vain. A once in a lifetime opportunity gone with the wind, leaving me in the dust to spend my entire life regretting the decision. And to make matters worse, the orphanage doesn't keep you once you reach eighteen. I would have been thrown into the streets to fend for myself."

"Not true," replied Isaac, "you know we would have helped if it came to that."

"I don't know that! You never spoke to me for three years, Isaac! *Three whole years.* You abandoned me all because you lost in a rap competition."

"That's not true –"

"I tried to get in contact many times, but you ignored all my messages," Luke's eyes watered, "I looked up to you like an older brother. Not once did I think you would become Cain when I became Abel to achieve my dream. We even vowed to not let a girl come between us, but then you go let a competition do so. I thought you would be proud of me, but clearly I was wrong . . ."

"It's not like that, bro. It's Nick . . ."

"I don't understand," said Luke.

Clearly the agent had no intention of relaying any of the messages given by Luke. He was more toxic than Isaac originally thought, "Nick bribed the judges, Luke . . ."

"Not this again!"

"It's the truth," Isaac's hands were stained with blood, but he got up and stood firm, "you can either go ask him, or even ask the judges."

"If that's the case, why spend the whole Sunday trying to prevent me from speaking to them?"

"Because I don't think they have the strength to face you without confessing. You've become a global star, Luke. Your dream of rapping would be ripped apart if this were to get out. Bro, you got to believe me, I was doing it for you."

Was Isaac telling the truth? Had Nick really bribed the judges? All this time . . . Decep Records deceived him?

"You . . . you're lying, Isaac . . ." Luke tried to convince himself, "just be honest and admit it . . ."

"It was six months ago . . . six months ago the judges gave their hearts to the Lord and confessed everything."

It could actually be true. Nick bribed the judges? All this time . . . Luke Chase lived a lie.

The celebrity's knees were weak and couldn't hold his body any longer. "For six months you never said anything . . . I thought I had the skill. I thought I finally beat you . . . I thought I was talented . . . how foolish I was."

"You are talented, bro," Isaac ensured Luke, "I don't care who says otherwise . . ."

Now wasn't the time to be optimistic, "Isaac . . . who else knows about this?"

"The two judges told brother Ryan and his wife," he said, "they then called my mom, and she told me. It was decided such information leaking would just put you in a bad spot, plus you were innocent in all of this. There was no need to bring your name down."

"Thank you . . ."

The lights of vehicles pierced through the darkness and revealed the scene. The sirens relaxed, but not the flashes of red, blue and white.

"NCPA! Don't move!" yelled an officer, "put your hands where I can see them!"

Isaac obeyed. Luke stayed.

"His hands is covered in blood!" alerted a familiar voice.

"It's not what it looks like!" said Isaac.

"Quiet! And *you*," the officer spoke to the celebrity, "put your hands up now!"

No response.

It was the officer from the accident that happened last week, the one that spoke to Isaac's mom. Isaac relaxed as the possibility of being shot decreased, "Bro," he whispered to Luke, "put your hands up."

"Why is he not responding?" Officer Dave asked Isaac.

"I don't know," he replied.

The medical staff were amongst the cops. Luke was in his own world on his knees as if in silent prayer.

How much had Nick kept from him?

"We don't have any weapons," said Isaac, using his body to explain, "the kid over there has been shot and I think they both in a coma."

"Stop resisting," said another officer, "turn around and keep your hands where I can see them."

"Did you not hear me?" he turned towards the Officer he knew, hoping that *he* would listen, "the kid's been shot! Help him!"

"Do not move!"

The need to rebel tried to overtake Isaac. How could they focus on him when the kid could die?

"Don't try anything stupid, son," came another voice, like an older version of Dave's.

Isaac's wrists were chained together. The Captain gave the medical team the go ahead and the males on the floor were tended to. Both ended up in hospital.

"Luke Chase? It's you again . . ." said the Captain. "What have you got yourself into this time, son?"

"Are you arresting me, sir?" asked Luke.

"We pretty much only taking you and your friend in for questioning."

"You know, I won't be able to perform for your daughter if you arrest me."

"What are you trying to say, son?"

"We didn't do anything," replied Isaac, instead.

"Then you got nothing to worry about," the Captain, himself, snapped Luke's hands together. "You've got the right to remain silent."

+++

"Do I get to make a call?" Luke finally got to ask.

"You pretty much won't need a lawyer if you're innocent, son," said the Captain, assuming that like everyone before him, the celebrity would phone to seek legal advice.

"Yeah, it's all good. I'm not worried. I just need to have a conversation with my agent."

"Your agent can't talk his way out of this one. He has less power here than a lawyer . . ."

Luke chuckled, "I hope you're right, sir. I really hope you're right."

TWENTY-THREE

THE ROOM was beyond plain. The walls were an endless white. The cuffs no different than before. The chairs hard, might as well been rocks.

"Then you guys came and the rest is history," said Isaac.

"You really expect me to believe that, son?" said the Captain, with a tone willing to make accusations.

"Whether you believe it or not, sir," replied Luke, "that's how it happened."

The Captain eyed them both, but they challenged him blow for blow.

"How's the kid?" asked Isaac, concerned.

"He's critical, but stable," said the man in charge.

"So he'll make it?"

"Most likely . . ."

A knock on the door startled the young ones. The Captain was like one of those teachers that ignored the sound to leave, for he dismissed you, not the bell. He wanted confessions, but he wasn't going to get any. He pretty much decided to put the stares on hold and left without another word.

The best friends absorbed the atmosphere of being arrested for the first time.

Isaac never feared it. He was prepared for the coming persecution promised by the Messiah. This was only a taste.

Luke wasn't afraid of walls. The people inside were the problem. Surely Payton's death would be broadcasted all over the city. Surely one of them would come to avenge their fallen brother. Surely . . .

"You get to use your one call?" asked Isaac, curious to what the agent would have said.

"Yeah . . . you sort out the car?" asked Luke.

"Yes, my mom's going with Mrs. Rennells to fetch it. You'll get your phone then . . ."

"I'll be gone by then."

"Gone?"

"Nick's still in the state."

"Oh . . . does he know?"

"Yeah, but not that I'm arrested," said Luke, "apparently there are videos on social media and he wants to talk to me about my contract."

"Where are you going to meet him?" asked Isaac.

"At his place, or at least the address he gave me."

"You want me to join?"

"Nah, I'm all good."

"What you going to do when you find out it's true."

"*If* it's true . . ."

"Bro -" started Isaac, but was cut off when the Captain returned with back up, "New evidence has been found," he said, "videos have gone around social media showing the incident. And we would bring shame to our name if we couldn't figure out that Payton shot the kid."

"Luke's reactions were crucial in this situation," said Dave.

"Yes," agreed Isaac. "He saved my life."

"Yes, he did," said a woman, "if Luke Chase hadn't interfered with Payton Rogers, you would have been shot in the head Isaac Banner. Instant death."

All eyes flew her way, but nothing was said. Riley Sanders, said her name badge.

"I'm currently working on the Grand Fortuna Case," said another officer, with eyes on the celebrity, "so I'm starting to think that Luke just likes punching people."

The former suspects laughed at the accuracy of the comment.

"We pretty much managed to get the videos banned," said the Captain, "the gun used by Payton was ours. It got stolen when our colleagues were ambushed at the scene of an accident."

"I remember seeing that on the news last week," said Isaac.

"Yes, it was on the news, Isaac Ban –"

"Some of us got places to go and people to see," Luke interrupted Officer Sanders. He turned his focus to the Captain, "Are you going to release us or not?"

"We just want to let you know that you will be performing Friday after all, and that Payton, who is in a coma, is currently under investigation," replied the Captain.

"Take heed, Luke Chase," said Officer Sanders, "Payton Rogers may lay an assault case once he wakes up."

"That's if he remembers anything," mumbled Luke as they freed his wrists.

+++

Mrs. Banner ran into the North City Police Station dripping tears. Isaac's heart ached and tears steadily climbed down his cheek. He hadn't seen his mom's eyes so red since . . .

Now wasn't the time to think about that. They drifted into each other's arms like puzzle pieces, "I'm so glad you're okay, son."

Hearing his mom's words threw him overboard. He couldn't say anything, but the flowing river of tears said enough.

"Wasn't Luke with you?" she finally asked. "Please tell me he's okay . . ."

Isaac managed a nod.

"Our Captain is currently taking Luke home, mam," said the secretary, "nothing to worry about."

Taking him *home*? She ignored it and took Isaac home rather. If Luke was with Oscar, surely he'll be fine.

+++

"Don't you want to call it a night and go home?" asked an officer.

A car pulled up in front of a massive house. Way too big for one person. The lights were on in every room as if each were occupied.

Why hadn't Nick invited Luke to crash here rather than the hotel? *Liquor.*

"Are you pretty sure you want to do this, son?" the Captain asked this time.

"Yeah, I'm sure . . ." said Luke.

No one was convinced.

"What? You don't believe *this* story either?" he added.

"No, we believe you," the Captain eyed the house, "trust me, *I* believe you. Just one thing though, when you question your agent, ask him for the paperwork on your wages. I want to go through them."

"Why?" the celebrity asked, curious.

"Look at this house, no agent earns this much," said Officer Den from the back seat, "the bribery you claim happened is nothing compared to him low-key stealing from you."

"With all due respect, sir, have you seen the crowds I please? Just ask the Captain's daughter."

"That's my half-sister."

"That's even better then, easier access," said the celebrity, oblivious to his usage of words. "If I'm beyond rich, shouldn't my agent be too?"

"Don't get us wrong, son," clarified the Captain, "agents do earn a lot of money, so much so, if you hadn't mentioned the story, we wouldn't suspect anything. But now . . ."

"You suspect he's stealing money from me because of the bribery?" Luke put it all together.

"Indeed, we do," confirmed Officer Den. "A person like him would do anything to get what he wants."

"The wire is online," said another officer from the back, "you guys are all set to go."

"You ready to do this . . . pops?" asked Luke, putting their plan of deception into motion.

"Please don't get use to calling me that," the Captain got out of the car. "Can't have my wife thinking I cheated on her again."

Nick Dobe opened his front door to find Luke Chase and some older guy on his door step. The agent was no way dressed for visitors.

Luke's "father" recognized the agent, "Good evening."

"Good . . . evening . . ." Nick barely got the words out.

"May we come inside? It's pre - quite chilly out here, wouldn't you say?"

The agent welcomed them inside, but his brain still tried to process the person in front of him. He had seen him before. But where?

"My son has said so much about you." A hand was stretched out, "it's so good to finally meet you, Nick Dobe."

"Your son?" the agent shook it firmly, "Luke's *your* son?"

His client had a fair father? It was possible, it explained the celebrity's lighter than usual skin. But why now?

"Yeah, I can't believe I actually found my pops," said Luke, "I plan on revealing him to the world on Friday."

"And the mother?"

"She's . . ." Luke stopped.

"She's dead . . ." said his father.

"Sorry to hear that . . ." Nick consoled.

The ticking clock filled the silence.

"I'm sorry for appearing like this," said the Captain, "if you want me to leave -"

"No, it's not that," said the agent, "Luke has been like a son to me, seeing his *real* father is just overwhelming."

"I understand -"

"Nicky!" came a voice from upstairs, "come play with us!"

"And you seem to have company," added the Captain.

"My girlfriend -"

"Nicholas!" came another voice, "don't keep us waiting . . ."

"Her cousin . . ." said Nick, "please take a seat, I'll be with you shortly."

The agent followed the voices.

"He probably recognized me already," the Captain said to Luke. "Why would you say that?"

"I'm pretty much a guy that's hard to forget, and he was at the Grand Fortuna Arena, remember?"

"Yeah . . . I actually forgot about that . . ." confessed the celebrity. "Dispatch."

"Ain't it too soon?"

"They'll wait outside –" the Captain was cut off by Nick, who came with a bottle and a glass for each, but no contract.

"Thank you," said Luke. "Can we get down to business, Nick? When I phoned earlier, you said you had good news for me."

"And I do have," he poured into the glasses, "it actually calls for a celebration."

"I don't drink on the job," said Luke's father.

"The job?" asked Nick.

Was Luke's father part of the NCPA? No, it couldn't be. They don't work in casual clothes.

"My pops' a financial manager," said Luke quickly, "that's why I phoned you. I would like him to take care of my money going forward."

"What's wrong with me doing it?"

"Nothing, uhm . . ." Luke stumbled.

"We think it will lessen the load on your plate," suggested Luke's father.

Was this man pretending to be Luke's father? It was highly possible. Why else would he want to manage the money, other than to steal it? Nick had to somehow warn his client before it was too late . . .

Throughout the tour, Luke was very desperate to know if his parents were still alive. He hoped they would show up to one of the concerts, even searched. The celebrity was easy prey for some money hungry crook. But how could Nick possibly ask for a DNA test without causing a scene?

"I've been handling it just fine up until now," he replied.

"May I see it then?" asked the Captain.

"See what?"

"The paperwork."

"Paperwork's up country," said Nick, moments before a sip of his drink. "I ensure you that all is good."

"Well, if you insist, then it's fine," said the Captain.

Just like that? Maybe Nick was wrong about the man.

"What about the contract?" asked the celebrity.

"Yes, here's the good news," Nick downed his glass. "Decep Records has changed it to a two album contract. In which you will have two separate tours. More money this way."

"And the bad?"

"It will be over a six year period rather, not a seven."

"I don't find fault in that, do you, pops?"

"*Nah*, we all good, son," replied his father.

"What about content?" Luke asked.

"The same. Money makes the world go round, kid," the agent guided their eyes to the Platinum award. "Giving them what they crave is how you make it in this industry. It's that simple."

"Is that why Isaac wasn't signed?" the celebrity added.

"Who's Isaac?" asked Nick.

"My opponent in the final three years ago."

"We had strict regulations three years ago."

"Only the winner would be given a contract? Really?"

"Don't act surprised, Luke. You knew this . . ."

"But you said that you would have signed me regardless of whether I won or not," Luke countered.

Nick was trapped in a corner, "You must have heard me wrong, kid."

"That must have been it. You need to open your ears more, son," said Luke's father. "Can I see the room you staying in?"

"Room?" asked Luke.

"Haven't you been staying with Nick?"

"In the contract we agreed to put him in luxury hotels," said the agent.

"Why luxury hotels? That's *pretty* much a waste of money."

"Because he's a celebrity and has way too much to keep track of it all," said Nick. The word, *pretty*, reminded him of someone, "By the way, I never got your name, Mr . . ."

"NCPA."

"NCPA?" Nick finally got the revelation of who was in front of him, "North City cops?"

"You are under arrest, Nick Dobe."

"But I haven't even asked about the bribery," said Luke.

"Bribery? What's the meaning of all this?"

The door was kicked in as the house was flooded with officers.

"We have reason to believe you've been stealing from your client, Nick Dobe," said the Captain, "you have the right to remain silent."

And so the agent exercised his right. He confessed to nothing the whole night behind bars. Until the dawn of a new day. Only then, Nick Dobe requested to speak to his client, Luke Chase. And what a morning it would turn out to be.

THURSDAY MORNING

THE HIDDEN GENRE

TWENTY-FOUR

THE ROOM, itself was already cold. The terms and conditions made by the agent were no different. "That's the deal I'm willing to make with you, kid," he said.

"I don't like the sound of that," replied Luke. "Why don't you tell me everything first? Then I'll decide what's going to happen going forward."

"I don't like the sound of *that*," said the agent, "it puts everything in your hands."

"Which I'm starting to think is about damn time!"

Nick's lips froze. He wouldn't give anything away just yet. He needed assurance to not being locked away, but Luke wasn't budging. The celebrity seemed to be on some sort of premeditated mission. As if no matter what the agent said, he wasn't getting out of this one.

The Captain and a few colleagues were dissecting all that was being said from outside. The NCPA couldn't do anything unless Luke laid charges. So leaving him alone with someone like Nick was risky, but the celebrity was optimistic. He believed he had the agent in his back pocket. Thanks to Oscar, all the Force could do was wait and see.

"Okay . . ." the agent finally surrendered. "What do you want to know?"

"Why me, Nick?" asked the celebrity.

"Why you?"

"Why choose to play around with my life?"

"I was not playing around with your life, kid. You have serious talent."

"Then why not trust me? Did you think I was going to lose the final?"

"That doesn't matter, cause you are the artist *I* wanted –"

"You not answering my questions," said Luke. "Should I remind you that your fate is in my hands, Nick?"

"How so?" the agent asked, hoping for Luke to mess up somehow.

"Your house has been raided and the paperwork has been found."

"Oh, you can't be serious," an officer got upset. "I know he's a rapper and all that, but surely he should know what *confidential* means?"

"I wouldn't let it get to you, son," said the Captain, who seemed to take a certain interest in the celebrity, "Luke Chase has the agent where he wants him. Just watch . . ."

"I was not made aware of this," Nick was raged inside, but kept calm.

It could be true. The paperwork wasn't up country like he said, they were in the safe at his North City residence. A warrant would easily grant them access to it. But Luke could be lying about the raid. No, Nick couldn't risk it. His client dropping the charges was the only way out. He had to obey. And if that didn't work. He had a gift Luke couldn't refuse.

"I want your word that you'll drop the charges like you said," he continued. "I'll answer whatever you ask."

"Do you think Isaac won the competition three years ago?" asked Luke, ignoring the request.

"This again?"

Luke got up to leave.

"Okay, okay, sit down, kid," Nick couldn't stall for a breakthrough any longer.

The celebrity gave his agent side eye.

"Yes . . . Isaac won that battle three years ago. Are you happy now?" asked Nick. "You know, if it gets out that you won via bribery, your reputation will be destroyed."

"I already have that covered," Luke sat down. "For the first time you the one that's late to the party. Not that you need to know, but I have another agent organizing something for me."

"You firing me?"

"I ask the questions," said the celebrity, "not you, Nick."

Agent Dobe shifted as if trying to find a comfortable spot on the rock.

"I hope he asks my question," said the early officer, no longer upset.

"Your question?" asked Officer Riley. "How would Luke Chase possibly know what question you want to ask?" she got no reply. Stupid question from her side. "What was your question?" she asked rather.

"Why were you involved in what happened at the Grand Fortuna Arena?" Luke asked his agent.

Nick's eyes enlarged quicker than his heart panicking, "Who . . . who told you I was involved?"

"The guy I knocked out confessed to everything," Luke used what was now a new profession of his, lying.

"I swear there was no intentions to kill you, Luke," added Nick quickly, "I have no idea why he threatened you with a gun. It was meant to be a quick in and out mission. But for the first time on tour, you decided to have a drink before a show. Everything would have gone real smooth had you gone to drink after the show; as you usually do."

"You call me, losing my voice, a job well done?"

"You wouldn't have stayed in this state had it happened. We would have taken you back East to get your voice fixed. We could have avoided all of this," the words came easy to the agent.

Luke on the other hand was lost for words, "I'm struggling to believe you would do something like this to me . . . I looked up to you like the father I never had. But everything was a lie . . . did you even speak to the CEO?"

Nick's eyes found the floor. "No . . ."

"I can't believe this . . ." said Luke. "What's so bad about my home town that you're keeping me away from it?"

Nick's forehead frowned, but he glared into Luke's eyes, "You don't know?"

"What don't I know?"

"About Ruth?"

"Oh, I figured it was you who deleted her number from my phone. And then you got the nerve to tell me not to answer unknown numbers." He admitted, "I still don't know the reason though."

Nick said nothing.

Something was wrong, they weren't on the same page when it came to Ruth. What was Nick referring to, if not the phone?

"Luke . . . I listened to you when you spoke, kid. It's the reason why I kept you from North City. You kept talking about how family was important. How you would one day find the right girl and not abandon your children like your parents did you. I listened to your words, kid."

Luke said nothing.

"That's why I'm surprised Ruth hasn't told you," continued Nick. "You're a father, Luke."

+++

The news outlet, Isaac watched, reported a shootout between gang members in the courts. The morning was filled with false witnesses claiming more than one shot ripped the peaceful night away from them.

"The videos being banned is all the proof we need," said one, "they're hiding the fact that these courts have become a battleground for the gangs. The Ryvils and Yutors are constantly at each other's throats. It's always the same thing over and over again. We not safe here anymore."

Their competition, North City News, reported that the NCPA continues to insist on the fact that there was only one gun shot. They said to have eye witnesses to confirm it.

"Is it true that the incident involves Luke Chase and his agent?" asked a reporter of one of the other outlets.

"Well, that pretty much depends on how you perceive it," replied the Captain, outside the police station.

"Agent Nick Dobe tried to have his client, Luke Chase, assassinated."

"What?" Isaac nearly choked on his hot chocolate, "Come on, you can't be serious?"

"Why are you even watching *this* channel?" asked Mrs. Banner, while her son recovered.

"I think you need to go back to your studies, son," said the Captain, "if *you're* the future of journalism, then I don't have hope for it . . ."

The TV went off the moment Oscar walked off screen.

"I was watching that, mom," said Isaac.

"No, you were staring at it and subconsciously sipping hot chocolate," said Mrs. Banner, "plus, what makes it worse is, you know the channel is filled with a lot of fake news, yet you still sit there and watch it."

"That's the exact reason why I watch it," Isaac put the cup down. "I know the truth, mom. I was right there when everything happened. I guess, I was hoping that hearing the lies would make me laugh and forget it for now."

"And then what?" she sat down. "After you've had your fun, you still have to face the truth, Isaac. You know this."

He more than anyone knew it. Still, Isaac stared at the screen as if it would recognize his face and come to life.

"I'm here if you need to talk, son."

Isaac kept at it as if he insisted that the screen had seen him before. Mrs. Banner took the empty cup and informed her son of an upcoming hot chocolate special.

"It's all my fault," he finally said before his mom got to the kitchen. "If I hadn't responded to Payton's lies, everything would have been fine. I thought it was the situation of Jesus calling out the Pharisees and scribes. But now I'm starting to think it was a Satan tempting Yahshua type of situation. And I fell for it."

"You're wrong," his mom snapped the kettle on.

"It's the truth, mom, why should I continue rapping when all it does is cause friction –"

"And you think Jesus came to make peace? No, He came to make war . . . " Mrs. Banner joined her son on the couch, "I can guarantee you that if you ask any artist out there, they will tell you that they've had haters, and if not haters, set backs. You can't please everyone nor can you make the right decision every time. In the moment it may feel right, but the consequences soon follow after. Worst thing is that, even if you don't make a decision, and someone has to make it for you, there will still be consequences. Why would you want to suffer from someone else's decision when you can learn from your own?"

Mrs. Banner was going to leave it at that as her son seemed to be in a world of his own. "Remember when Jesus said that the truth sets us free," she continued instead, "yes, He was referring to Himself, but I've been living for a few decades now . . . don't laugh at my age. I've noticed that the truth can set us free in life as well. So before you make such a decision on your life, allow God to work in this situation. You may see an outcome you weren't expecting once the fog clears."

The kettle screamed in excitement of another cup, but that had to wait. There was a knock on the front door.

+++

Luke knocked and knocked. He had no patience. He wanted answers.

How could Nick do something like this? Why hadn't Ruth mentioned something like this?

"Luke?" Mrs. Rennells opened the door.

"I've come to see my kid –"

Dishes fell in the kitchen. Alongside Ruth.

+++

"Good morning, mam," said the courier. "Does Isaac Banner live here?"

"Yes, that's my son." Mrs. Banner was so confused from the courier's lack of a drop off package that she asked, "Is something wrong?"

"No, nothing's wrong, mam," he replied.

Isaac popped his head by the door exposing his shyness.

"And you must be Isaac!" the courier had a massive smile, as if talking to a child. He pulled out an envelope, "This is for you! May you two have a great day ahead!"

"What is it?" Mrs. Banner finally asked.

"An invitation," replied Isaac, "but to what?"

TWENTY-FIVE

Breaking News:

Luke Chase leaves Decep Records!

NORTH CITY News, Radio & Visuals broke the tragic news to the world. Tammy's source was none other than the celebrity himself. He sat head in hands. *Liquor.* Was it the correct decision? He would find out in due time. Right now it seemed to be the right call.

Luke, the source, asked Tammy if he could be kept anonymous, which he found amusing. He wondered how nervous and upset the officer must have been after Luke spoke of *confidential* matters with Nick. It didn't matter though. The cops got a confession and Luke found out that he was a father. With emphasis on, *was* . . .

Ruth had fainted earlier. The words, that came from Luke's mouth, surprised her beyond reason. She never thought she would ever hear them. It pleased an old part of her, but the memories flooded her brain. It was too much at once. Thankfully, there was no need to rush her to the hospital for any injuries. The same couldn't be said about the dishes.

"Why now, Luke?" Mrs. Rennells had asked. "It's nearly been three years since Ruth tried to contact you."

"You won't believe me if I told you," he had replied as he took a seat in the lounge.

"Try us," Ryan had said after he laid Ruth down on her bed, "we would love some answers."

The celebrity told them what his agent had said about answering the phone, deletion of the number and how Nick never mentioned anything about the conversation he had with Ruth. He knew that Luke would have returned immediately had he found out. Therefore the agent kept the news to himself.

"And now I've finally come to see my kid," he concluded.

Mrs. Rennells' eyes had watered while her husband avoided eye contact, as if it would make the statement go away.

"Can I see him?" Luke had asked, "or *her?*"

There had been no response.

Did they not want him to see his kid? If so, he wouldn't allow that. Luke would be there for the child. He would not be like his parents. He promised himself that.

"Luke –" started Chantal.

"She didn't make it," Ruth had said to everyone's surprise.

"Ruth?"

"She didn't make it, Luke," she said once again, softer.

"Princess," Ryan ran to support her, "you should be resting right now."

"I'm fine, daddy, let me be here when you tell him."

"Tell me what?" Luke had asked, "What do you mean she didn't make it?"

Luke was too young for this kind of pain. He wasn't ready to hear it, never mind what happened to his parents. Ryan would have kept the information from him had the celebrity not insisted on what happened to his one and only child.

"Stillborn," Ryan tried to lighten the word, but it was too heavy. And reality hit Luke hard.

The Rennells' had shed their fair share of tears, but witnessing Luke's come down broke their hearts.

"We have learned from a trusted source that agent Dobe has been stealing from his clients since the beginning of their contracts," said Tammy on NCN, "but he profited the most from one client in particular, Luke Chase."

He sat there motionlessly listening to Tammy report what he had told her. A tear rolled down his cheek at the thought of it all. Luke lost his first child. The kid was never going to suffer what he had gone through. He would prove himself to be a better father than the one he never had. He would treat his child the way Mr. Banner treated him. But that chance was now gone. All thanks to Nick. A *gift*, is what he had called it. Clearly he didn't know about the *whole* situation.

Luke understood Ruth's situation, and no blame had gone her way. She was overly excited when she found out she was pregnant, but just as overly terrified.

Her older sister had waited until marriage before having a child. She wasn't clean though. Ruth knew that Casey slept with her boyfriend long before they married, but what their mother didn't know, wouldn't hurt her. It was their secret. Plus, Casey was careful, she never got pregnant.

Whereas Ruth found out she was pregnant really late, and thanks to a random check up. She showed no signs whatsoever; one of those rare cases. Luke was the only person she slept with. Where? She couldn't remember, but things went too far at the celebration party. He became her first, there was no doubt that he was the father. But Nick got to the phone before Luke during a recording session. Ever since then, Luke hadn't answered one unknown number. And Ruth's life went down hill from there.

"We have gotten in contact with Luke Chase himself regarding the next statement," said Tammy.

Luke gave the screen side eye.

Was she going to break her vow and reveal the celebrity as being their source?

"The Rappers Behind Bars competition that happened three years ago was rigged," she said, "Luke Chase, who found out recently, has confirmed this to be true. He is deeply sorry to his supporters, but ensures us that he was not involved in the bribery. He thanks everyone for their support."

"Thank you, Tammy," Luke laid back, and his eyes settled on the ceiling.

"The judges have confirmed the bribery to come completely from Nick Dobe," she continued, "Decep Records claim no involvement in this, saying that Nick was acting on his own. Reactions from the industry as a whole has been mixed. Some side with Luke Chase for leaving and wish him all the best. Others think he should have kept his mouth shut. They believe that Decep Records made him the person he is today and that he should have been grateful, for not many get such an opportunity. Luke Chase has been called a disgrace to the industry. But that's not what Isaac thinks."

The TV grabbed Luke's eyes.

"Mainly known as Yahshuandi, the Gospel Rapper, he was the opponent in that famous final three years ago. Isaac has responded briefly through an email, and this is what it says: 'I do not hold anything against Luke, and I believe he is a very talented artist. We both did our best to win the competition. It's a shame that it got rigged when it could have gone both ways. I'm proud of him for stepping out like this, not many would do so. May he Luke, Chase and Conquer for Christ going forward.'"

"Why am I not surprised?" Luke chuckled as his eyes settled on the ceiling again, "I know you think I'm talented, bro. I appreciate that, I really do. But I've got to prove it to myself this time."

+++

The CBM store was dead. Hardly customers roamed the aisles in search of content through books and music. Then again, it was kind of hard for Isaac to tell when he was fixated on what the ceiling had to offer.

"Hello," said a customer.

"Good afternoon," Ruth brought Isaac's eyes down to earth. "I see you into rock music, mam."

"Yeah, I can't get enough of it," said the young woman, "I'm trying these guys out though, but I'm ultimately a huge fan of Stellar Kart. Do you think they any good?"

"I don't listen to rock, but Far From Home, Ashes Remain and Nine Lashes I notice from my mom's playlist," replied Isaac, "I don't know about the last one though."

"Red is a huge band on the Christian charts," added Ruth. "They not like Stellar Kart, but you can rock with them."

"Great! I'll take all four," she said and smiled at Isaac, "and next time I return, maybe you can take me through the type of music you listen to."

The customer left, but Ruth's eyes never left her. Isaac was back at it with the ceiling.

"She's friendly," said Ruth, sarcastically.

"Can't wait for her to return," replied Isaac, subconsciously.

"Oh, wow," said Ruth. "So what? You can show her Reconcile and Corey Paul's song?"

"Ooo you?" asked Isaac. "That's a good idea actually."

"Oh, wow."

"I don't know what to do, Ruth."

"Isaac, are you for real right now?"

"Yes," he said, "I honestly don't know if accepting the invitation is a good idea."

"I can tell you now what will happen if you do accept *her* invitation."

"Her?" Isaac's forehead wrinkled, "I thought the invitation was from Luke."

"Oh, wow," Ruth was embarrassed. She immediately put two and two together though, "Yes, the invitation to the *competition*. I think you should accept it."

That answer was too quick for Isaac's liking, "What if it's another trap he subconsciously set?"

"I don't think it's a trap. I think it's a genuine attempt to have a proper winner this time."

"I never looked at it that way," Isaac got lost in his thoughts, "a proper winner . . ."

"Think about it for a second, there will be eight rappers with each being a Christian Hip Hop artist," said Ruth, "some will be from our country, some abroad. For one, all the judges are from abroad, apparently the MC as well. He said that you will recognize the judges immediately."

"He said?" asked Isaac, as if that was all he heard.

"Yes, I'm sorry I forgot to tell you. Luke came to the house earlier," she went on to explain the whole mix up regarding Nick, her and Luke. The call situation made sense to Isaac, as the agent clearly held back messages he wasn't supposed to, "I get it now, why he didn't understand what I meant by forgiving him. It was never his fault to begin with."

"I'm really sorry to hear about the kid, Ruth," said Isaac as if this was the first time the topic came up, "I'm strangely glad he didn't know about her."

"Me too, Isaac," a tear escaped her eye. "Me too . . ."

They held onto each other. Neither let go. Neither said anything. Both drifted into eternity. Why *couldn't* they stay like this forever?

"We have work to do," he confirmed why, "but you should have taken the day off."

"Oh, wow, you sound like my mother right now," she replied, "speaking of which, she says you should join us in the competition."

"Us?"

"Yes, I'm going to face my fear, Isaac," she said, smiling, "people only know me for my singing because I'm too scared my rapping won't be nearly as good. I'm going to get on that stage and defeat my fear once and for all. Whether I win or not, doesn't matter. I would have conquered my fear for my Elohim. Maybe you should do the same."

There was murmuring in the store amongst staff members.

Was it because Isaac and Ruth were breaking the rules of no contact in the store? Abusing their power?

No, they had a visitor . . .

"My brother," said a familiar voice to Isaac, "I would listen to her if I was you."

TWENTY-SIX

WHILE THE man's eyes were on the couple, he stood there with triple the amount on him.

Was this Isaac's brother? The staff knew about Ruth and Casey, but there wasn't even a whisper about an older brother for Isaac. Now he stood here in the store? And on top of it, he was a well known artist.

"C:map?" said the couple in unison.

"Did we not discuss this already?" asked the man. "Using my stage name in a normal conversation feels weird. Imagine I called you, Gospel Rapper, every time we spoke."

"Sorry, we didn't mean to," said Isaac, "we're just surprised to see you, Claude."

"No worries," he replied, "I'm just as surprised as you."

"How so?"

"You know, to see you not wearing a gown in public."

The artist got a giggle out of Ruth, "I will never forget that night."

"Trust me," said Isaac, "that was a one time thing."

"Really? You then looked so attached to it," joked Claude. "There's no harm in that, fam."

"I agree," added Ruth.

"Stop it, guys," laughed Isaac.

"I know it's only been a few days, but it's good to see you guys again."

"Likewise," said Ruth.

"Weren't you and Johnny scheduled to leave yesterday already?" asked Isaac.

"That was the original plan, but then the strangest thing happened. Myself and Johnny got an invitation, and . . ."

Claude's words drifted away as Ruth thought about that night she ended up at Isaac's place.

She had knocked countless times hoping for him to answer. And he had. Ruth wanted to jump into his arms and express what she was feeling, but Isaac hadn't fully overcome his shyness yet.

"Ruth?" he had asked, "Are you okay?"

She had been invited inside, but declined. The Uber waited outside, and he was expecting a guest. At least, that's what Ruth told him.

"You need a lift?" she had asked Isaac.

"A lift?"

"I'm on my way to the concert," she said, "thought you might want to tag along."

Her inner voice begged Isaac not to question. She was hanging over the edge. Hearing Luke's name would only have sent her over. And he did just that. He hadn't asked.

Ruth's eyes and the Uber was enough evidence to come to a conclusion. "I'm no way dressed for a concert," Isaac said instead.

"It's okay," mumbled Ruth, "I understand . . ."

Why was he so shy when she needed him the most?

Isaac needed to man up, and he did just that. He grabbed a pants and the sneakers he had left by the door. The gown matched them, so it looked low-key planned. But there was no time to fetch a jacket, so what he had on had to do. The rope was ripped out, but it fooled no one; it was no unzipped coat. It mattered not, Isaac was going to be with Ruth tonight. If she wasn't concerned about the appearance. Why should he be?

They had arrived at the concert with all eyes their way. C:map found it amusing. The fans paid to see him on stage, but their attention was on something completely different. He had just finished a song about standing out in the world. It seemed planned to the crowd, for entertainment purposes. Some cheered at the uniqueness, others laughed. But there was no malice and Ruth was by no means embarrassed, clipped to Isaac's side. In fact, she hadn't felt so happy in years.

"That's exactly what I mean about standing out," Claude had said, "presented by the Gospel Rapper himself."

DJ Johnny relaxed the instrumental and Claude gave him an exciting look of *it worked.*

"You the man," DJ Johnny's lips read as he pointed to the rapper with a smile.

"He's the man that Elohim used to reach me," Claude announced, "come join us on the stage."

"No, I couldn't," said Isaac, drowned by the noise, "this is your concert."

"I can't hear you down there," he had replied. "Why don't you come closer and say it?"

The cheers were deafening, but Ruth's smile was what convinced Isaac. They made the journey towards the stage.

"Let me tell you something while he makes his way up here." Claude said, "Elohim used him to bring me to the true side of music, and more importantly, the true side of life. But the funny thing is, even as I speak to you guys right now, I still don't know this guy's real name."

"And he has a lovely lady with him too!" DJ Johnny had announced to a roar from the crowd. Something about couples always gave humans an extra boost of energy. They were given mics and asked to introduce themselves.

"My name is Ruth."

"Isaac Banner . . ."

"Let's give it up for Ruth and Isaac Banner!"

The crowd blew the roof off the place. Ruth had flushed at the thought of having Isaac's last name. This was the very place where the Gospel Rapper had lost the final all those years back. It was without doubt a nightmare back then. But now he stood with the girl of his dreams.

Would he trade the final for her? Never . . .

"Guys, are they not cute together? I mean, come on," the artist stood on the edge of the stage, "can all the couples in the building make some noise!"

C:map sat down on a speaker after the crowd calmed down. He looked at his best friend, "Yo, Johnny, you'll have to forgive me for this, fam. You see, I can't help but notice all the love in the building." He turned to the crowd again, "You know when I sing, I gotta use some of that auto tune, but Johnny! Wait till you guys hear his voice! You'll be blown away."

"What?" DJ Johnny was as surprised as the crowd.

"This guy's hiding from us!"

"Really, Claude?" asked the DJ.

"Don't get all shy on us, come join me as we give them a song from the upcoming album."

"DJ!" yelled the one side.

"Johnny!" yelled the other.

"They waiting for you, DJ - Johnny," said Claude, with the rhythm of the crowd. "It's not good to keep people waiting."

"Yeah, but great things come to those who wait," joked the DJ. He was replaced in the back and took to the stage. Isaac and Ruth made their way into the sea of humans.

"I'm going to get you back one day for this," Johnny had promised with a smile.

"Surprise me . . ." said Claude. He turned to the crowd, "This song is called, Comparisons. It's for all the lovely couples here tonight."

(C:map)

You like a pearl
You are my, girl
You've been molded and folded
And slowly you've become my, world

You like a dream
You are my, queen
You've been magical, beautiful
Slowly you've become every, thing

205

(DJ Johnny)

And I? I'm longing for the days
Just you and I
I've fallen for your ways
The day you caught my eye
I'm trapped in this game
A game they call love
I long for your arms
Like separation's way too much
I thirst for your touch
I just can't get enough
I've had my fight with lust
So I know that this is love
I know that this is love
I know, this is love

(C:map)

You like a book
You got me, hooked
So romantically, mystery
One kiss is all that it, took

You like a charm
You got me, calmed
With your fragrance and patience
And somehow I knew I was, gone

(DJ Johnny)

And I? I'm longing for the nights
Just you and I
In the dark you are the light
No second passes by
That I'm not thinking of you
And what you mean to me

THE HIDDEN GENRE

This world tries to hold me down
But with you I am free
My heart beats for you
Sometimes you don't see
The battles I face everyday
Just for you and me
You haven't left my mind
So I know that it's meant to be
I know that it's meant to be
I know, it's meant to be

(C:map)

I heard your friends say they like me
And your family down the same road
Girl, I will never take you lightly
We make heat when the world cold
You like a pearl found in a dream
An understatement: you mean everything . . .
You like a charm found in a book
An understatement: never thought we would . . .
At first, it's so inviting
Every get together so exciting
Hate it when we fighting
But this go make us stronger
At last, you know that I won't blow it
May not say but I sure show it
I am here so we can grow it
But this go make us better

(DJ Johnny)

Comparisons, I use
No way to described you
And all you do

Comparisons, I choose
No way I can hide you

THE HIDDEN GENRE

And all you do

Comparisons, I use
No way to described you
And all you do

Comparisons, I choose
No way I can hide you
And all you do

(C:map)

You like a pearl
You are my, girl
You've been molded and folded
And slowly you've become my, world

You like a dream
You are my, queen
You've been magical, beautiful
Slowly you've become every, thing

You like a book
You got me, hooked
So romantically, mystery
One kiss is all that it, took

You like a charm
You got me, calmed
With your fragrance and patience
And somehow I knew I was, gone

During the song, everyone blurred out to Ruth and Isaac. The people were swaying figures in the corner of the couple's eyes. They entered each other's soul's as they had done before, but this time, Isaac had the courage to stay.

He wanted this: a moment where he could freely confess his feelings without doubt. He would confess with his lips, but he had no intentions of using words.

She needed this: a moment to truly find out whether Isaac was man enough to take on a real relationship.

It was now or never. He had to make a move and stick to it. Their eyes locked. Isaac's hand grazed her smooth skin as he made his way to her jawline. The nerves throughout their bodies were overreacting. And her body gave in, shivering at the touch. Slowly their lips connected like the years of preparation. Soft. Slow. So enjoyable. Everything Ruth had craved. Everything Isaac had wanted. It lasted longer than the years leading up to it. And the wait was worth it.

Ruth's body tingled at the memory. Isaac's name sang from her tongue ever since.

"Yes, Ruth?" Isaac asked, "Ruth?"

"Yes?" she managed.

"You called me?"

Oh, wow, had she said his name out loud?

"Ruth?" he asked, again.

Oh, wow, she had.

"It's nothing . . .," her brain searched for an excuse, "uhm, just give it thought . . . the competition's on Saturday."

"Will do, but regardless," he planted his lips on her cheek. "I will be there to support you."

SATURDAY NIGHT

TWENTY-SEVEN

C. H. H. AIN'T DEAD:

THE HIDDEN GENRE

IT WAS here at last. All the excitement built up throughout the past few days exploded with fireworks. The competition was over promoted as if it was going out of style. The tickets were made affordable for everyone and the event was hosted at the Grand Fortuna Arena.

Decep Records, who cut ties with the celebrity, refused to refund the fans who bought tickets for the North City concert. They swore it was a request done by Nick to make money from an artist that should have been on vacation in the city, not performing. Luke Chase alongside his new sponsors, who couldn't be more prouder to be involved, covered the tickets with a ten percent extra. A token of gratitude.

Social media was the driving force for fans excited about the competition, but no one knew who the judges were. Luke Chase insisted that they only be revealed on the day to encourage fairness. This move met a lot of criticism due to the celebrity's knowledge of the judges, considering he was indirectly involved in the current bribery scandal. Half the contestants were just as top secret as the judges. It was a known fact that Luke Chase hosted the competition, but whether he was in it or not; was another mystery.

The crowd amazed at the opening performance by the group RMG featuring Deraj with a song called, Respect That. The song was old, but the fire was still burning bright. Next was Young Bro featuring KG Santiago with their song, In His Freedom. The dancing vibe was electric. Some fans were being introduced to artists hidden in plain sight, like the genre they represented.

"Let me do the honour of welcoming y'all tonight," said the MC as he stepped out to a roar, "the name's Datin and y'all know I've been saying it for a while now, but tonight, y'all go see that *C.H.H. Ain't Dead!*"

Cheers echoed throughout the arena. It was filled with family, fans, critics, Christian artists and secular artists. North City News, Radio and Visuals were given the honour to present it to the world. Tammy respected the agreement made with Luke, and because of it, she was rewarded with a dream come true for her career: a worldwide audience.

"First, before we begin," Datin glanced over the crowd, "I've been asked by Luke Chase to tell y'all that this competition, *C. H. H. Ain't Dead: The Hidden Genre*, is dedicated to the one and only, Mr. Banner, who many may know as Ivan Banner, one of the most respected rap rock artist to date, a legend in his own right!" He let it resonate with the crowd, "These are the direct words of Luke Chase, and I quote, 'He was a father figure to me and he played a vital role in my life. I will never forget that, nor will I forget his words, 'Books is more than ink on paper, like Music is more than words, my son. Looks would scare if you could see deeper, like Rubiks' seem complicated at first . . . until you solve one.' You will always be in my heart, uncle Banner. Thank you . . .'"

Mrs. Banner's heart melted at the impact her husband had on Luke's life. It was just like the man she fell in love with, always helpful. Chantal comforted her best friend who let out nothing but tears of joy.

"Onto the competition!" announced Datin, "first, many have been waiting to find out who they are. And now that we here, let me introduce our three judges for the night. Let's give a shout out for KB! Eshon Burgundy! and Bizzle!"

The judges walked out to an applause. They were huge artists in the small part of the industry. These guys were respected and most of all, Isaac knew them. This competition would not be rigged. The winner would be rightfully chosen.

"Oh, if you thought Christian rap was soft, you go learn today!" said Datin, "now before we bring out our contestants, let's welcome one of the finest DJ's around. Give it up for *DJ Johnny* on the ones and twos!"

Johnny came out to an applause he had never heard before. A stadium nearly packed with people. It was ground breaking.

"Okay, y'all ready?" asked the MC. "First up, we got our DJ's partner in crime, *C:map*!"

There was an uncomfortable vibe amongst some of the people. Claude was a known secular artist regardless of his recent statements. Some swore that this competition would expose him once and for all. Just like they believed Luke Chase would be exposed. It was the only reason many came. To witness it . . .

"Next, all the way from Asia, *Yourz*! plus, she brought a friend with her too, give it up for one of the *Uchiha Disciples*!"

The two artists came out not long after each other, with the latter being a school teacher, music being a hobby of his. There was a small group of learners who had flown down to support him, courtesy of Luke Chase. They were all dressed in their Uchiha red and black uniform.

"Following him, is a man known in Europe for his skill, give it up for *Bloodline*!"

As much as Luke was breaking world records with his sales, this artist was breaking European records with his. The man didn't have any personal family or friends in the crowd, but he was surely known and respected by many. He even had fans in different sections of the stadium.

"Now, last but not least, the locals," said Datin, "give a shout out for *Ruth Rennells!*"

She received a massive cheer from the supporters. People heard her story of using this competition to overcome her fear of rapping in front of people. She was one of the few that was announced into the competition, and this made her an inspiration for females wanting to step out. Her family was in full attendance, including her older sister, Casey, and her family.

"Next, she is well known here for her battling, let me hear it for *Mkay!*"

Many knew her, but not as much as Ruth. This was ultimately based on the social media presence. It didn't matter though, Ms. Miller, Joe, Gabi and her family were there to support her. Plus, Margarette being here meant that she was slowly getting through to Luke. One step at a time.

"Man, I can already see tonight's going to be memorable," said Datin, "let's give it up for a finalist of the Rapper's Behind Bars competition, *Yahshuandi, the Gospel Rapper!*"

The local favorite stepped out to a roar of support. Ruth gave Claude a nod of acknowledgment. She had set the foundation, but ultimately he had convinced Isaac to be here for more than just her supporter. Isaac stood on the stage ready to act on his purpose for living.

Datin said nothing. He turned to the rappers on the stage as if counting to make sure there was enough.

Was that all the contestants? Where was Luke Chase? He hosted the competition, why wouldn't he be a part of it? Wait, there were only seven. They needed one more rapper. Would it be the celebrity?

"And the final contestant," Datin finally said, gaining relief from the people. "*Young Chaser!*"

"Young Chaser?" they questioned, now more confused than anything.

Who was he? No one ever heard of him before.

Gabi looked to Ms. Miller for help, but her eyes were firmly on the stage with no elements of surprise, as if she expected it. Who would've thought Mrs. Lonely knew an apparently famous rapper?

A smoke bomb blew at the entrance to the stage, startling everyone.

Was it a terrorist attack? Or an attack from one of the gangs perhaps?

The smoke cleared slowly as if it found pleasure in messing with everyone's nerves. There Luke Chase stood, or was it Young Chaser? Gabi didn't know anymore. That was a lie. She did know, but couldn't fathom the fact that Luke, her favorite artist, was right in front of her at the orphanage, and she hadn't recognized him. She had to strip herself of the self-proclaimed number one fan title after such a revelation.

"It's like Sasuke's summoning jutsu," whispered the Uchiha Disciple, he bowed in respect, and the students followed suit.

"And these are the eight contestants for tonight's battle," said Datin, "in order, C:map, Yourz, Uchiha Disciple, Bloodline, Ruth Rennells, Mkay, Yahshuandi, the Gospel Rapper, and Young Chaser."

Although slightly confused with the host's new stage name, the crowd cheered for the lineup that was about to entertain them. Ruth was the underdog, so she was being monitored, but no one could deny that most of the eyes were on Young Chaser. And he wasn't even expected to win.

"This is how it's going to work," said Datin, "we'll start with the local based Eight-Claps for the quarter finals. However, the decision will be made by the judges, not the crowd." Disappointment spread throughout the stadium, "Now now, before y'all complain too much. Imma explain why and y'all go understand. This stadium is massive, and although not all fifty thousand seats are filled, majority of them are. The reason why such a rule is applied, is to bring fairness to those who don't have majority of the fans sitting here tonight."

The people thought it through and understanding occurred among them.

"The four with the most shots will be declared the winners and will go into the Semi-finals! Y'all ready?"

They were ready, but the noise wasn't proof of it, "Nah, I don't think y'all ready at all," said Datin, "if that was the case, y'all wouldn't be so soft. I can barely hear y'all from here!" The MC stepped to the edge of the stage, "Let me ask again. Are y'all ready for some heat!"

The crowd was beyond pumped up for the competition and it was time to begin.

"Let's do this!"

DJ Johnny dropped a dope beat for anyone who dared to take the first crack at it. A mic fell from the roof and hung there like a bungee jumper with no one to pull him up.

The host stepped up first.

TWENTY-EIGHT

YOUNG CHASER stood there with his eyes firmly on the crowd. The instrumental ripped through the arena. Many were here to see him fall. He would prove them wrong.

The people bumped their heads to the beat. The contestants' hearts pounded in their ears. Luke came out last, so everyone expected the order to be likewise. But he wrapped his hand around the mic and began on the following drop.

(Young Chaser)

Let me start and make this hard to keep up
For I have changed the way I view the cup
See that's half full with the Messiah's Blood
And it came upon sinners like the flood
We grow in it - so the Word can never be outdated

Jesus would have used a plane to preach to the masses
And even if His body had to end up being cremated
He would have still went about rising from the ashes

The rapper owned the beat, but it continued like it dared others to try the same. He glanced at Isaac as if tempting him to respond, but the opponent didn't flinch. Luke was expected to have a go at the end, not immediately.

Many thought him to have a *save the best for last* attitude, but this wasn't the case. In fact, he made the situation much more difficult now.

Had he humbled himself by going first, or was it an arrogant move to make it harder for others to keep up? If the latter was the case, the other contestants, being rooted to where they stood, made it a win for him.

"Y'all may go at anytime," said Datin, "but keep in mind that we don't have all night."

Not just anyone could respond to such, and avoiding it wouldn't help either. The Gospel Rapper felt the eyes in his path, as if the crowd deemed him the only one worthy to challenge Luke. If not Isaac, who?

"You can't please everyone nor can you make the right decision every time. In the moment it may feel right, but the consequences soon follow after. Worst thing is that, even if you don't make a decision, and someone has to make it for you, there will still be consequences. Why would you want to suffer from someone else's decision when you can learn from your own?" the words of his mom slowly pushed him forward, step by step, but then Claude took a stand himself.

The artist knew what he had to do. Elohim used him to speak to Luke with the *Purpose For Living* track, it was only fit that he responded to this as well.

Claude turned to Isaac and gave him a nod. He would sacrifice his rap to set things straight with Luke. The bars were good. But they had no deeper meaning behind them, at least, compared to prophecy they didn't. If Young Chaser studied properly, he would have known exactly what the Messiah came to do.

The mic was swaying side to side waiting for a victim, but no, the next rapper would not become one.

(C:map)

You're right! However I will still sit among you
But let me give a much clearer view
Virgin birth - perfect life yet betrayed
Sent to the earth so we can be saved
I understand your points but check prophecy
Came to preach to Israel and started in Galilee
No broken bones and there's much more
He didn't come to destroy but to fulfill the Law

Things were heating up. The crowd didn't get the artist they wanted, but the reply they needed. Support was not withheld from the brave artist. It was encouraged. There were no rules about battling as long as it contained the Word. Claude scored big time, to a point that the doubters were slowly believing in his transformation. The tension in the air thinned out, and this gave the others confidence to move to the mic.

DJ Johnny made a shift in the instrumental adding extra rhythm to the hi hats with a new bass flow banging. Same sample. Different rapper.

(Uchiha Disciple)

Haters all around - three-sixty Byakugan
Predicting these haters like I got the Sharingan
Living out my life a follower of the Son
Man, they can't resist me cause I'm a Royal One
Haters all around - I'm still hating none
Snakes lurking but I caught them with the Rinnegan
Lord, help my unbelief on which the enemy feeds
That fruits of the Spirit come not from mine but Your seeds

The rumors were true. He really was part of a group of people who were huge Naruto fans, as well as massive followers of the

Word. Many criticized the stage name chosen, yet the creativity used in the way he mixed the two could not be denied. Although the rap was legendary, a lot of people in the crowd never understood some of the lines. This was due to a lack of knowledge, or due to a lack of interest in anime. But they weren't the judges, and this by no means gave the rapper a disadvantage.

Three rappers already went. Voluntarily stepped forward and impressed the crowd. That complicated things for the next contestant.

Regardless, Ruth stepped to the center. She didn't know why. Her body just moved on its own. Excitement or adrenaline? Probably both. She checked the sea of eyes, but couldn't hold firm. Everyone was looking. All eyes locked on her as if she was the only girl in the world.

What were they thinking? Did they want her to step up, or did they want her to choke? Could she do this? She never sang in front of half this amount of people, now she had to rap. Was she expecting too much of herself? Was this even worth it?

"You got this, Ruth," a familiar voice reassured her with a hand on her shoulder. "I know you can conquer this fear. You sure inspired me to conquer mine."

Isaac reached out and gave her hope when she was drowning in her thoughts. It was short, but it was sweet. And sometimes in life, it was the small things that mattered. Ruth was going to prove that fear was nothing but mental illusions.

(Ruth Rennells)

I know this life go bring some difficulties
But You said that You go defeat my enemies
And I'm tempted to disobey what the Divine said
But I fight this battle with a spiritual mindset
Father reach people through this competition
Make them see that this is more than religion
Use the lamb to replace the beef
For we have a purpose - no oxygen thief

She stood tall and owned the instrumental with her man by her side, just like he promised. Truly Isaac was a man of his word, someone she could rely on.

The fourth person to take on the mic left, and although Ruth was close to becoming one, there were no victims . . . yet.

Whether witnessing Ruth, overcome her fear, gave Margarette the courage to step forward or not, didn't matter. She was on a mission herself. Mkay glanced at Luke, the judges and then the crowd.

Was she going to challenge someone? Was she going to challenge Luke?

The rapper took control of the swinging mic on the drop of a new beat.

(Mkay)

True prayer is more than words
Some say prayer is a two way process
Actions of it be like birds
Take a risk to fly and discover progress
You believe in God and the whole world knows you don't mumble
But even the demons believe in God and tremble
You live in luxury letting your faith get to your head
Yet your tree ain't fruity and faith without action is dead

She had done it again. Margarette dedicated the rap to herself and Luke. Four lines each. Those who knew her personally weren't surprised. She hadn't hesitated before. What would have stopped her now?

Luke didn't understand what the woman's problem was. The whole point of getting her number was to ask her, but then the creation of this competition stole his time. Enough was enough. He had to speak with her, face to face, backstage as soon as possible, before things got out of hand.

The European stepped to the center. The instrumental got comfortable in the listeners' ears. Bloodline took the mic and looked to the sky for guidance. He never rehearsed any lines. They came to him naturally as he freestyled, what he believed, God wanted him to.

223

"Tell me the lines you want me to use, Elohim," he whispered to himself.

(Bloodline)

Fearing the unknown, but I think it's just my empty excuses
Cause like Moses, I'd still follow the path the Lord chooses
They always trying to win, but backwards like crosses and noughts
Hate someone? You've already committed murder with your thoughts
Fear? More like Face Everything And Rise
So I stand strong waiting for Satan's demise
How I struggled? Came a long way with the fam eating from a single bowl
They cause trouble, so I'm blind to the world like a golden mole

The crowd wasn't ready for such heat. The judges gave points to each rapper. But Bloodline went and set the bar high again. The last two rappers were Yourz and the Gospel Rapper.

Could they top that? Would Isaac step up to make it easier for the woman from Asia? No need. She was a regular at overcoming odds in her country. She believed this to be no different.

(Yourz)

Go Japanese on you, you better respect my Kami
All I do is get higher, let the water cleanse – tsunami
Check, I ain't Jesus, I can't take two and five and feed a thousand
Check, I was struggling, yet Jesus helped me top the mountain
Brothers hated on me like Joseph
But it's our Father that gave me the robe
Couldn't handle my dreams like Joseph
But I endured all my struggles like Job

She was proud of her bars and the way she presented them, but the people were comparing her spark to Bloodline's fire. She would have lost if it were between the two of them. But the judges had the final decision.

Isaac walked to the mic while the beat danced in the background. He looked upon the faces, and they stared back.

Was the rumors about him true? All the tourists had to go on was his last competition three years ago.

DJ Johnny increased the volume slowly, and slowly the sample built up until it dropped the bass.

(Yahshuandi, the Gospel Rapper)

Man shall not live by bread alone, But by every word from the mouth of God
Take on all with Elohim my backbone, But you shall not tempt the Lord your God
Cause for My namesake, without a doubt, you going to suffer persecution
But we won't break, as we go all out, for the truth will not be hidden
Listen, do not lay yourself treasures on the earth
Don't even chase pleasures - know your worth
But what you know about walking on water, out the boat with the Son of Man?
If you so focused on paper, wanna be the goat, but the greatest is then a lamb!

Rumors about Isaac's style of rap had spread throughout the lands. And now they had witnessed it themselves. He mixed the words of Yahshua with his own, but they flowed like living waters. The rapper plagiarized as if it wasn't a crime to do so, but it had some Christian artists wondering whether they plagiarized enough.

"If you thought Christian rap was soft, you sure learning today," said Datin, "the judges will go tally up the scores, but don't go anywhere y'all. Our next performance will keep the heat going."

The judges went to tally up their shots at the back, away from wondering eyes. A. I. The Anomaly kept the crowd warm with her song, Miss me. King Allico and Constance took to the stage to perform their song, Confident.

Datin returned to the stage, but the results hid in an envelope. The announcement of the semis was up next, but the fans didn't know if they wanted it or not, like picking a favourite amongst favourites.

The contestants semi circled behind the MC while he glared over the crowd. Some people were extra nervous as if certain rappers winning would benefit them more than entertainment. But the question still remained: Who was through to the next round?

TWENTY-NINE

WHO WOULD go to the semi-final?

C:map, Uchiha Disciple, Ruth Rennells, Mkay, Yourz and Yahshuandi. They all waited anxiously on the stage. Young Chaser was calm, as if he knew the four finalist personally. The way the people went on about, Bloodline, he must be a guaranteed top four if not the winner. The crowd was silent waiting for the MC to call up the names.

"Okay, y'all," Datin held an envelope in his hand, "the names have come in regarding the four that are through to the semi-finals. Those that are on this list are the ones with the most shots. However, not in any particular order. Remember, just because you part of the first four mentioned, doesn't mean you through to the next round," warned the MC. "I will declare the winners in the order of my choice. Are y'all ready?"

The crowd attempted at a cheer but the nerves got the best of them.

"Seek first the kingdom and everything else shall follow, I want y'all to remember that," he looked at each rapper that stood before him, "even if you don't win tonight, remember why you did it in the first place. Don't lose the passion. This competition doesn't guarantee you anything but exposure. Yes, the winner would have a greater chance of being signed to a label, but it isn't a guarantee. You could go home right now, but still be approached by someone longing to promote your sound. My opinion, I see talent and potential in each and everyone of y'all. Stick to your roots, and y'all go far."

The contestants nodded in gratitude for the acknowledgement, but not one had any intentions of going home first. Not with the world watching. This was the time to be recognized by a label, and going home doesn't exactly count.

"When I call your name, please step forward," said Datin, "Yourz."

She stepped forward with not even a hint of satisfaction. The people in the stadium were on the edge of their seats wondering if she would be going through.

"Uchiha Disciple, please come forward."

There was gasping amongst the supporters. Were they going to take the first two spots? Were they about to leave the bigger known artists battling it out for the last two? Some of the students thought that was the case, that their teacher was into the next round, but they were calmed down by the other supporting teachers as if they were still in class. All eyes fell on Datin.

"Thank you for your participation, but this is the end of the road for y'all."

The crowd was left speechless, but some murmurs managed to escape the mouths. Whoever, in the history of competitions, told two contestants to step forward, and then sent both, not one home? The two rappers bowed in respect to the MC, the people and last but not least, their fellow Christian artists. They were cheered off the stage.

Yourz was all right until she stepped out of sight. Realization hit her and tears fell like a cloudburst. The Uchiha Disciple, more experienced of the two, had to comfort her.

She had overcome so much in her country before she got invited to promote her music in a competition that would have a worldwide audience. Lyrically, Yourz wasn't far off compared to her fellow artists, and she would only get stronger from this. The talent was there, and as long as she used it, she wouldn't lose it.

The Uchiha Disciple had no problem with the loss, but the disappointed kids hurt his heart. He came to share his love of the Word and anime. The kids came for the excursion more than anything. They would be leaving tomorrow evening, but they still had much to explore in North City. Each second available would be spent wisely.

The MC looked up at the now, six, slightly nervous artists in front of him. He asked them to stand a bit closer to each other, ensuring that no one would bite.

"Next up," he said, "C:map, please step forward."

What was Datin planning? The last shall be first was a very well known saying from the Bible. Was that what he was going for? Would the last four mentioned be the top four into the semi-final? Claude thought so, until . . .

"Yahshuandi, the Gospel Rapper, please join the front."

Surely Isaac wasn't part of the first four losers?

Luke Chase was nervous for his friend. He wanted victory over him, but not like this. He wanted a one on one battle. A pure, no conspiracy, victory.

"Congratulations, you two are through to the next round," announced Datin.

The crowd made their mixed feelings known, but ultimately were happy for the local favourite.

Not even bravery was enough. What did C:map have to do to prove himself to these humans? Nothing, he didn't live to impress them. But why couldn't they accept his decision to become a Christian?

Luke Chase had caused a lot of stir with his one day good, next day bad type of attitude. Why was it easier for them to quickly assume he was another Paul situation, yet doubt Claude's transformation?

The two finalists congratulated each other on the progression with a solid handshake.

"I would be careful if I were you," tested Datin, "the first semi-final is between the two of y'all."

They wished each other all the best regardless and this pumped the crowd up for their battle.

"Ruth Rennells, please step forward," continued the MC.

It was the moment of truth. There was two spots available.

Had Ruth achieved more than what she planned to? Did she make it into the semi-finals?

"Mkay, you may come to the front."

There was a loud scream from one of the girls in the stands. It caused some startled smiles, but Margarette was grateful for the type of friend she had in Gabi.

Isaac was taking on C:map in the next round, was she to take on Ruth? Two male and female battles? What condition would this type of loss leave Luke in?

"Y'all ladies were brilliant tonight," said Datin, "but only one can go on in the competition."

Oh, wow, Ruth was still in it. A fifty percent chance to go through, but there was still a chance.

Casey always said, *all you need is zero comma one percent certainty to work on a case.*

Yes, this had nothing to do with detective work, but the overview idea of there being a chance of her progressing in the tournament was good enough. The MC hadn't sent her and Margarette home like he did the first two, so who knows.

Ruth overcame her fear already, some would say that was job well done, let's pack up and be on our way, but going on to win the entire competition would be even more so special. It would mean that she didn't just overcome her fear, she annihilated it.

"And the one going through to the semi-final is . . . Mkay."

Gabi led the celebration for Kane.

Ruth had lost, but ultimately won her battle against fear. She couldn't be more prouder, however the crowd's applause made it greater. She didn't have to win the competition to feel like she annihilated it. Her standing in front of everyone was all the proof she needed.

The opponent congratulated the winner and took leave.

"Next up, we have Bloodline and Young Chaser," said the MC, "please step forward."

The ultimate decision was kept for last. Half the crowd waited nervously in anticipation. The others were ready to protest on short notice. Would Bloodline, arguably the winner of the round, go through, or would the host and his reputation be put through?

The two rappers glanced at each other as if weighing each other out. Bloodline had no expression across his face as if he knew who the winner was. But Young Chaser had a grin on his face as if he too knew who the winner was.

Were they both correct?

Luke understood that the guy next to him must have realized that it was over. He was good. A worthy challenge. But he was up against the one and only Luke Chase. And the celebrity could rap on any beat like Mr. Banner.

Why would someone from Europe think they could ever stand up to someone like him?

"Both rappers have the potential to do wonders, but unfortunately as you know, only one of you can face Mkay in the other semi-final," said Datin, "the judges have added the scores together and believe this to be a fair decision."

It was so obvious who the winner would be. Datin holding back was all for entertainment purposes. Mkay versus Young Chaser was what the fans wanted to see. They wanted Luke to get revenge for the stunt Margarette pulled at the church. There was no better platform for a semi-final. It was like the agent, he put behind bars, said, *"Giving them what they crave is how you make it in the industry. It's that simple."*

"The one going through to the next round is . . . Bloodline!"

THIRTY

THE WEATHER, news and the people were all stunned to silence. Not murmurs, not rumors not even conspiracy theories were able to form on the lips of those watching. Bloodline, who was expected to advance, didn't hint at any form of celebration as if he hadn't heard the announcement.

The celebrity, for the first time, got punched in the face. Not only did the MC leave him for last. There was no confirmation whether he lost because of C:map or this foreigner. "What do you mean, *Bloodline*?" asked Luke, too stunned for the thought of *Liquor* to cross his mind . . .

Datin showed him the list of four names. First was Bloodline, Yahshuandi, the Gospel Rapper, Mkay, and then C:map. Young Chaser wasn't even considered as an alternative.

The winner let out a smile at the realization that he won the entire round. Cheers went around the arena like the Mexican wave as if this was the evidence they needed to silence the critics. C. H. H. Ain't Dead: The Hidden Genre was not a competition that would be rigged. The winner would be chosen fairly.

Luke Chase stood on the spot as if he was waiting for someone to tell him that it was all a prank. He was actually the one through to the semi-final, in fact, he won the entire round. But no one confirmed it.

Had he really lost in the first round? Had he lost in the beginning of the competition he hosted himself? How was this possible? It had to be a dream, nah, it was a nightmare. Luke closed his eyes to suppress it.

"If you not part of the top four, could you please head back stage," he heard Datin say.

The celebrity opened his eyes and everything was still the same. He was still the person everyone waited for, but they weren't waiting for a performance of any sorts. It was humiliation in its truest form.

Luke finally walked off the stage with his lip hanging on the floor. He had to accept the result, but the competition wasn't over yet. Isaac gave him a pat on the shoulder, but it was as if he became oblivious to everything around him.

Isaac's dream was shattered when he lost three years ago. He remembered all too well how awful it felt. Although the experience was not exactly the same, was Luke going through a similar feeling? Would he distance himself too?

"Don't let it get to you, fam," said Claude to Isaac, "it will take time, but he'll get over it."

The semi finalists were presented to the world. Tammy continued to broadcast everything to those who had television, and those blessed to get themselves to a radio.

"Going into the next round will be different," said Datin, "it will be C:map versus Yahshuandi, the Gospel Rapper and Bloodline versus Mkay. This round will require sixteen bars on the beat that DJ Johnny produces. First, we'll give our contestants a break and after that, the first match will begin y'all."

Antwoine Hill, Bryann Trejo and Nino Salas stepped up to perform their song, On Fire. And if that wasn't enough, 1K P-Son, 1K Phew and 1K Don Tino followed up with their song, Slide. The One-Sixteen Clique also came through with Illuminate to present their own unique sound to those that stayed seated instead of getting refreshments.

Ruth joined her family in the VIP section to watch the rest of the competition as a spectator.

"You did well, princess," said her daddy.

"I'm proud of you, Ruth," said her mommy.

"You always did only have a zero comma one percent chance of winning, but that should have been enough. Strange, isn't it? Now I have to sit here and support your cute boyfriend instead of you," said Casey, she ignored the eye roll from her husband. "Don't tell anyone, but I low-key thought you won the round."

"Of course you did," laughed Ruth.

Casey's younger sister greeted the rest of the family and sat with them in preparation for the semi-final.

How were they so . . . normal? Mrs. Rennells didn't know. There was no resentment, regardless of the fact that Ruth thought Casey was favored more. Maybe if Chantal had a sister, she would understand.

A roar of excitement echoed throughout the arena as C:map and Yahshuandi, the Gospel Rapper took to the stage. The refreshments made fans more hungrier and thirstier for the next round. The semi-final would begin shortly.

Isaac's eyes locked onto the sky as if he was impressed with the full moon's blood red glow. "Thank you, Father," he whispered. The artist glanced at the VIP section. That's where he would have been supporting Ruth if it wasn't for Claude. But now she was there supporting him from the stands. He turned his eyes to his opponent who nodded in acknowledgement.

Was he thinking about the encounter as well?

After all, Claude had surprised them that day. Isaac and Ruth thought he and Johnny had already left the country as scheduled, but as he would explain, they were invited to this competition as well.

The two artists had gone to the back room to talk.

"Other than visiting, what brings you to the North City Mall?" Isaac had asked.

"I had a feeling you would not be accepting the invitation after I saw the news," Claude had replied.

"You assumed that Luke sent the invitation as well?"

"Not necessarily, I work in the industry, therefore I immediately thought he got another agent to organize the competition. It's this new agent that's been behind these invitations. Plus, it's all over social media."

"That explains why I haven't seen it. I've been avoiding social media recently."

"Avoiding? I didn't know you *had* social media," replied Claude, surprised. "How come I haven't been able to find you?"

"You won't find me," said Isaac, "I use the store's social media profile. Why were you searching for me anyway?" he asked, genuinely curious.

"And you've caught me out. You were right, I did come here for another reason, other than visiting," he replied with a smile. It didn't matter how Isaac knew. "I came here to thank you personally."

"Thank me?"

"Like I've mentioned before, Elohim used you to bring me to Him. I was a tasteless Christian during my high school years, you can ask Johnny, he was almost on the same route. But we still kept certain values from the Word due to growing up in it. In other words, we were lukewarm Christians."

"Many young followers go through that struggle."

"I think it's because of the routine of only getting the Word in on a Sunday at church."

"That sure plays a part, as well as the stereotype of only older people living the Word out."

"And I probably would've joined that list when I got older," Claude had said, "being an upcoming secular artist, that Rappers Behind Bars competition was a good way to spot future rivals. But then I watched you and Luke Chase make waves in that tournament. Honestly, I didn't think you guys would get past the first round."

"Trust me," Isaac had laughed, "you weren't the only one."

"Yet you proved us wrong."

"Only because Elohim saw it fit that way."

"Without a doubt He was behind it all, because I ignored your raps until that final. Yes, it's true. That final was the game changer. And where I am now is all history, but I had to leave the country to make something happen."

"Tell me about it," said Isaac, "this country is filled with secular artists."

"And that's more reason for us to push harder," Claude had said. "How else are they going to hear the Good News? That's why we want you to join us."

"In the competition?" the Gospel Rapper had asked.

Isaac and Claude faced each other now here in the semi-final of a different competition. Both ready for victory.

Had Elohim used him to get Claude to His side, only for the rapper to end up helping Isaac make a crucial decision?

+++

How dare they do this to him?

Luke Chase would be the laughing stock of the industry. It's not like he wanted to win the competition, but this humiliation may be beyond repair. All he wanted was to defeat Isaac. He wanted to prove to himself that he deserved the last three years of success.

Why was everything saying otherwise?

Bloodline was on his knees in prayer when Luke entered the finalist's preparation room. The celebrity held two bottles of water as if he were offering the rapper a choice. They were both still water with different outward appearances. Both had the same added content.

Was this too extreme? Was it worth it? Could he have thought of another way? Nah, there wasn't another way. How ironic was this turn of events . . .

"Yours Father is the kingdom, power and the glory, forever." Bloodline turned his attention to Luke as if he knew he was there the whole time, "Water? That should do wonders for my throat. Thank you."

"You got a tear running down –"

"Sorry about that," he sniffed, wiped away the tear and then took the drink, "it happens when my flesh doesn't agree with the Spirit. You . . . you're nearly there on this road to Damascus. I'm grateful to be involved."

What was that suppose to mean?

Bloodline drank a quarter of the water with his eyes firmly on Luke's as if he waited for the celebrity to say, *stop*. When he didn't, the artist finished the bottle.

"I'll see you out there," said the finalist.

THIRTY-ONE

Next Battle:

C:map versus Yahshuandi, the Gospel Rapper

A CHILL dashed down the spines of the fans. It was C:map versus Yahshuandi, the Gospel Rapper. Both were honored to spread the Word. One proud to share the spotlight with the rapper that changed his mindset on music. The other proud to share the same light with the secular artist who wasn't afraid to spread the truth. Claude against Isaac would begin the moment DJ Johnny let the next beat rip through the arena.

"I don't think the crowd's ready for what's about to happen," said the DJ.

They tried to prove him wrong with their noise.

"Trust me," he insisted, "you guys ain't ready."

They increased their sound. The cheers echoed throughout the arena. Flashlights appeared within the audience slowly increasing in number as if mimicking the increase in volume.

Johnny got a sample ready, tempting the artists. C:map took charge patiently waiting for a drop, but the DJ hit a one-eighty making it a RnB slow love instrumental. The rapper got the first word down before laughter and confusion filled the arena.

"Did I not say I would get you back one day, Claude?"

DJ Johnny gave the sick beat attention again, but Claude hesitated to put words to the drop after his friend got revenge for the other night. He wouldn't do it again, would he?

The DJ had so much power with the push of a button. Johnny gave him a thumbs up though. He got his revenge, there was no need to do it again. Claude smiled and nodded.

(C:map)

Coming from school, we don't learn about religion
Taking Bible Studies away so we don't hear His wisdom
I got to live it right
I got to do it with precision
I was raised in Christ
But to surrender was my own decision
Watched by a crowd so I know there's temptation
Got my mama proud regardless of the situation
See we all made in His image
All part of His creation
But we continue to destroy
Like we were made for destruction
I trust Him like He asked me to and gave Him my burdens
Joy in the morning feeling like Moses when I split the curtains
Came a long way like walking through the Red Sea to get here
In God's land and He came down among us as simple as a server

C:map shared some of his testimony with a structure that was on point. Some of the crowd began doubting their doubt of the artist. Claude had proved himself over and over again. This rap was the cherry on top.

How would Isaac respond to it? Luke came to witness it for himself. The Gospel Rapper had a challenge and Johnny kept the instrumental banging hard.

(Yahshuandi, the Gospel Rapper)

When you close to breakthrough - the devil fights harder
And you don't need to get right to finally surrender
Look, the first four disciples were fishermen
Follow me, and I will make you fishers of men
Want me to worry about people talking about who I pick?
If you well, no need for a physician - I came for the sick
I did not come to call the righteous but sinners to repentance
False preachers? Watch the fruit and who chases possessions
For it's hard for a rich man to get into heaven
When it's easier for a camel to get through the eye of a needle
I pray you hear what I'm saying brethren
I told you three times who I'm going to bleed for
Saving the world with men, this is impossible
But not with God, for with God all things are possible
And the Pharisees are nothing but a whitewash wall
But He can change them too - look what He did with Paul

Not only the crowd, but Claude himself applauded the response from his opponent.

Young Chaser couldn't help but wonder who Isaac directed that to. Then again, he couldn't understand why he felt like everything everyone said was directed to him?

Datin took to the stage with the two rappers on each side. The judges gave their views on the battle and the Gospel Rapper was declared the victor. The people were proud and made their feelings heard.

Next Battle:

Mkay versus Bloodline

Datin invited the next two rappers up to the stage. Decision of who went first was left in their hands. Bloodline used his hand to gesture that the woman go first.

How kind of him, but Margarette was better at responding. She insisted her opponent kick things off and so he tried.

". . ."

What was wrong? There were no words.

". . ." he tried again.

Bloodline's voice was gone. The stadium was flooded with concern as he couldn't create one sound. Some spoke just to be sure that their voices were fine as if it could be an airborne thing.

How could this have happened? The rapper glanced at Luke, but didn't want to say anything, or was it because he *couldn't* say anything?

The medical team rushed to check on Bloodline, who fell to the floor. Luke lurked behind. As the host, it wasn't suspicious for him to be concerned, or at least, appear concerned about the contestant. It was decided that the finalist couldn't continue and needed emergency treatment.

"Emergency treatment?" Luke was stunned at the news. "How serious is it?"

"We don't know yet," said a medical staff member.

Could Luke have lost his voice completely from the stunt Nick tried? Nothing was said about the substance doing so much damage. This was terrible. Had he ended someone's career? Worse, had he ended someone's life? Was this the reason why the event manager hadn't returned his call? Was he too . . . dead?

Bloodline was taken back stage for a check up. Immediately discussions, theories and conspiracies broke out amongst the people.

Lathan Warlick offered to keep the arena occupied while they figured things out. The song, Tellem That I'm Coming, was performed as if part of Luke's master plan.

Datin checked around for a replacement and Young Chaser happened to be around. The finalists and judges all accepted the adjustment, and before everyone knew what was happening, Luke was into the semi-final. He would face Margarette Kane, a battle for fans around the world to witness. Mkay couldn't escape going first as her opponent was forced into second, but it was fine. She need not freestyle this one.

DJ Johnny flipped the beat under water and brought it back fresh like baptism.

(Mkay)

Left the state with the future in my hands
Nothing but successfulness in my plans
No worries when I'm able to keep my stomach full
Now I'm coming back empty like the prodigal
So much money just covering that emptiness
Started questioning and ended up finding Jesus
You'd probably stop me here with your foolishness

And Luke had. He had gone on to tell her that the industry wasn't for her. Yet, here she stood. Stronger than ever as if she had predicted the celebrity's immediate response to the name of *Jesus.*

(Mkay)

But God has the greatest faithfulness
My adoptive parents died when I was young
To the world it seemed like they still living
We went to church but didn't see the Son
Just in the motion like a cloud drifting
The wind controlling what we get to see
Keeping my focus on becoming a better me
They had my eyes and tears on the soil
Telling me to gain the cheers and lose my soul

Was she playing games with Luke now? Why would she talk about being adopted? Was she making fun of the fact that he wasn't? As if she was better than him? The joke was on her, he became a celebrity without the support of parents.

THE HIDDEN GENRE

(Young Chaser)

You died for me yet my knees don't want to hit the soil
I just did wrong and I do kinda feel ashamed in my soul
See I was told of Your resurrection and greatness
But typically I felt like I needed to witness
Only a wicked generation wants to see a sign
But even with the evidence I still feel the same
Now I know that it's not a mental but a heart grind
But is it really bad that I want the fame?
Walking into temptation like I can't control it
Got my eye on perfection but I can't hold it
I'm starting to notice what humankind lacks
While they trying to hide the historical facts
Father God, forgive me for I knew not what I did
Cause finding You requires no shovel to dig
See they trying to hide the truth for some reason
Telling us we hate but hell don't exist in their opinion

There was a terrifying silence in the stadium. Who won the round? It was a difficult question to answer.

"Please stand next to me as our judges make the decision on who will face Yahshuandi, the Gospel Rapper in the final," said Datin, sounding relieved that the choice wasn't in his hands.

"May I say something before a winner is decided?" Mkay asked, innocently.

Had Luke clearly contradicted himself in something he said? And if that was the case, was she going to call it out with the world watching?

"Go ahead," said the MC.

"Most of you know me because of the video in the church that went viral," she started, "but I ensure you what was said earlier by brother Ryan was much more important than that. It's been replaying in my mind over and over again. Now I know why. We all know that today is Saturday. Funny. Jesus asked whether healing someone on the Sabbath Day was wrong to the Pharisees. He also spoke the parable about the lost sheep. Today just so happens to be the true Sabbath Day as much as many think it to be Sunday. Today we will leave the ninety-nine to find the one. I surrender this battle to *Lukey.*"

Luke was punched in the heart by the only person who had the skill to lay one on his face.

"Lukey?" Datin asked, puzzled.

"Marge?" the finalist managed.

The fans couldn't help but share their confusion with the people next to them.

"It's not my mission to do it," Margarette gave the mic to the Gospel Rapper, "I believe God is going to use you to finally reach our friend. Make us proud, Isaac."

"Okay, I see it y'all. It has been decided," the MC announced. "The first ever final of the C. H. H. Ain't Dead: The Hidden Genre competition – Yahshuandi, the Gospel Rapper versus Young Chaser!"

THIRTY-TWO

YOUNG BRO and Bryann Trejo performed their song, For The Father, while the finalists were backstage in preparation.

"Why didn't you say anything?" asked Luke. The revelation was so unexpected to a point that he got defensive, "All this time, I thought you abandoned me. Why would you allow me to think that?"

"What did you expect me to do?" replied Margarette, more calmly. "Me being adopted was always bound to happen. I never thought it as abandoning you. Hearing you say that hurt me and I didn't know how to react . . ."

"I'm sorry . . ." Luke was ashamed. "I couldn't bring to life one memory other than your teachings of self-defense . . . I never thought I would ever see you again, Marge . . ."

"That's partly my fault. My adoptive parents couldn't wait for you to return from school for me to say goodbye. They had to be on the next flight home . . . and I didn't have the courage to tell them otherwise."

"I don't blame you for that . . ." he said, "all the scattered pieces have finally come together. For all I've said, unknowingly to your face, I ask for your forgiveness."

"Forgiveness given . . ." Margarette smiled as she opened her arms, "Hug?"

When they trained together at the orphanage, young Lukey would shyly ask for hugs from the older and taller Marge. She found it cute, even offered him a chance to kiss the part, he managed to hit, "better". It became their reward system, he would get a hug or kiss, dependent on what he managed to hit. And just like that, Luke had motivation to get better.

The now taller celebrity chuckled at the memory. "Only if you manage to get a body blow," he said.

"As far as I'm concerned," she replied, "my words already touched your heart."

The two embraced each other as they did back then. The warm fuzzy feeling, no different. The hugging stance, no different. The height of Luke, length of and the Chase of this hug, worth it.

"Ms. Miller told me what happened, Lukey," Marge said, once they broke away. "I understand why the situation could have been so misunderstood."

"It's just something I don't want to witness again, but I don't understand how I couldn't put two and two together," he found it amusing, "Marge is an obvious nickname for Margarette."

"I think your mind was still clouded by the abandonment issue, plus, I never told you my real name at the orphanage. There was no way you could remember something you never knew," the words softened the blow.

Luke Chase loved that about her.

"I came back to North City only to find out that you had gone on a completely different path already," she continued, "I myself had become a fan of the genre through my adoptive parents, however, their type of hip hop music was different to what I wanted to represent."

"Secular?"

"Your type of music, yes. I knew then and there why I discovered the genre the moment you had left it. I would be part of the people that God would use to bring you back, like the prodigal son." The artists finished their track on stage, "I know now that it's not for me to do."

"Are y'all ready for the final?" Datin asked from the stage. "Can we please have our finalists on stage?"

It was now or never. Although she never said it, Marge was convinced that he would lose, but Luke finally had the chance to prove himself. To beat Isaac fair and square. To prove that he deserved the last three years regardless of how it happened.

Isaac's opponent was on a mission. He didn't know if he were too. Margarette said that it was up to him to reach Luke. But how was he to do that?

"Here's how it's going to work," said Datin, "each rapper has thirty shots in which can be split, sixteen-fourteen, or vice versa. Young Chaser will start on the first drop by DJ Johnny. Time to show them the hidden genre, Christian Hip Hop Ain't Dead!"

The DJ dropped a heavy beat.

(Young Chaser)

I can't believe I made it to the final
But I ain't surprised it's against my rival
But is this a David versus Goliath?
Or a Satan versus Michael?
Since he masquerades himself as an angel of light
I promise this go be one hell of a fight
Took two L's yet I still made it
New in the Word so naturally I crave it
For it don't lose flavor eventually like gum
Like what was done on the cross cannot be undone
But why Jesus when there are so many?
Why few labourers when the harvest is plenty?
For He is the light when you are trapped in the dark
And He bit through His actions - He didn't just bark

The crowd was on the edge of their seats. Luke's round was pure flames. The people were nervous for his opponent. How would the local favorite respond to the international celebrity?

THE HIDDEN GENRE

(Yahshuandi, the Gospel Rapper)

I'm about my people, bread and about my goals
But I'm more about Yahshua - why He bled and how He rose

The instrumental went solo. Was he going about it the right way? Isaac looked to his mom as if she would give him the hint he needed. Her words replayed in his head.

Don't let it get to you, son, sometimes the words mean more once understanding is possible, Mrs. Banner had said after he lost three years back.

Was it possible now? Only one way to find out.

(Yahshuandi, the Gospel Rapper)

This grace is a gift I've come to cherish
For whomever believes in Him shall not perish
He is the Lord of Lord and King of Kings
Believe in the One sent by Elohim
Yet the fruit is how we know you with it
And avoid blasphemy against the Holy Spirit
For you still have time to truly commit to He who cares
For time is near when He will separate the wheat and tares
Understand to follow Him, you need to deny yourself
Take up your cross and forget about chasing wealth

The celebrity had heard these lines before, was it déjà vu? Nah, it was the rap from three years ago. The same one that his former agent said won the competition. Luke had "beaten" this before, this time would be no different.

DJ Johnny switched the beat to something lighter.

(Young Chaser)

He showed how to live a life that is perfect
He overcame death and disease like the opposite of morbid
Never promised earthly riches but He is surely worth it
And hell is nothing compared to that fiery pit

I was abandoned and felt like none can love me
But I never looked up to surrender to Him above me
Previous days I just sat back and watched life happen
Watching the world and trying to notice the pattern
Seeing violence and wondering where this God is
Finally noticed that our sin is the disease
Nowadays I will stand and preach life happened
But I don't know if I should thank Eve or Adam
As the devil made himself known in the Garden of Eden
But the One who can kill body and soul you should be fearing
As redemption took place when I started to lose hope
Do not be afraid, but believe! So I got out the boat

Confidence was pouring out of Luke as he gave Isaac room to respond. The celebrity may not remember all the lines of his opponent's rap, but he believed he set the bar too high for the Gospel Rapper to jump over.

(Yahshuandi, the Gospel Rapper)

Through Christ is how we are conquering sins
Through the Spirit we see a world of living skeletons
Or better known as the walking dead
And Christ already put the topic of public fasting to bed
For whoever does the Will of My Father in heaven is my brother,
sister and mother
So do not call anyone on earth your Father, for One is your Father
With His blood is how we have our new covenant
And the world doesn't understand the power in the New
Commandment
For we are to love one another as He has loved us
That includes the one who threw Him under the bus
For He gave up His life for us
In Yahshua the Messiah we put our trust
For He defeated death and rose on the third day
Showing He is God in the flesh and the only way

The instrumental cut out as if it was speechless, but Isaac had no reason to stop.

(Yahshuandi, the Gospel Rapper)

This world wants the lies but I'll give the truth instead
That we are the body and He is the head
So I tell you now that C. H. H. Ain't Dead
When the Living Word is being spread

The cheers would have blown the roof off the stadium had they designed it with one. Young Chaser fell on his knees as if the standing ovation increased the gravity on his body. The judges joined in and it was clear that a decision was already made. Luke put up a challenge, but it was too obvious he lost.

"We have our winner ladies and gentlemen!" announced the MC, "let's give it up for, Yahshuandi, the Gospel Rapper!"

SUNDAY EVENING

THIRTY-THREE

THERE HE stood, surrounded on all sides, unable to escape what he got himself into. A group this size would be embarrassing for the celebrity to perform for, so they sang to him instead. It came once a year, but for the first time in three, he shared it with friends and family.

The chocolate cake stood tall, on the table, surrounded by all types of treats, but none reached its glory. It symbolized Fortuna Island with the stadium being the center of attention. If that wasn't enough, the cake had the number twenty-one on it with one candle towering above every dessert offered.

This celebration took place at the Grand Hotel. They sang the birthday song that was arguably more famous than Luke Chase himself. It was a bittersweet moment. The track has and will out live him, therefore it was futile for Luke to challenge it. As the words floated throughout the penthouse from the lips of those who followed along, the celebrity was tempted to follow suit. He stayed strong until the end with a shy smile across his face.

"Thank you," said Luke repeatedly as if to each person in the room. "Thank you very much."

"Speech! Speech!" chanted the people, "speech!"

"Okay, okay," he replied, "only cause I like to give the fans what they want."

Chuckles filled the place.

"Oh man, where to begin?" he looked around for inspiration. There his rival stood, eyes on him.

"First make a wish," said Isaac, "and blow out your candle."

"How can I? I don't know what to wish for."

"Surely you can think of something," said Margarette.

The celebrity looked around, "I think everything I want is already here."

"Maybe not someone," she insisted, "but some *thing* . . ."

Marge had a point. Luke did want something, and he hoped his stay in North City would bring upon the desired knowledge. The birthday boy inhaled enough to blow out twenty-one candles. He let loose on the flame that was unable to put up a hint of a fight. Conquered.

"Speech!" said Ruth.

"Like father like daughter," replied Luke, "putting me on the spot in front of everyone." The celebrity kept his eyes on the Rennells' for a long second. They were in full attendance. "Family. I feel like I can call every single one here tonight, family . . . coming back home . . . this is the reason I came back home," he glanced at all in the room. "To celebrate this special day with those I truly considered family . . ."

"I'm glad to be considered such," said Isaac, to many nods, "I speak for everyone when I say we're glad to have you back."

"It's good to be back! I mean, the past three years has been a rollercoaster ride for me. I now understand why though. To think that so much happened in the shadows for me to have the spotlight, it's crazy. And I would like to apologize for everything," the celebrity sneaked a glance at Ruth, "but what I have come to learn is, we wouldn't be here so united if the events of the past hadn't taken place. I truly believe everything led up to this moment." Luke picked up his glass with champagne in it, "As I stand here today, I have been reunited with my sister, Margarette, from the orphanage, and my brother, Isaac, who has proven that he deserved to win the Rappers Behind Bars competition." The celebrity smiled, "Let's ignore who he defeated, and give a warm applause for him."

And so they did, led by Luke, himself.

"Come on, stop it," said Isaac as he made his way to Luke, "the real talent is right here, guys. Let's give it up for the birthday boy, Luke Chase! *Chase*, everyone!"

"Chase!" People shared the *chase* instead of cheers throughout the penthouse, each with the person next to them. Some went the extra mile to others.

"Let's relax and enjoy the night," ended Luke. He turned to Isaac, "*Chase*? Really? How corny can you get?"

"What? You think Luke! Chase! Conquer! Is Banner?"

+++

The night flew by like the past two weeks since he arrived in Amboria. He sat on the balcony where it all started. The Grand Fortuna Arena was visible and an inspiration for him. It stood out. A spaceship ready to explore the stars above. They, themselves, were in the sky trying to outshine each other.

"Beautiful, isn't it?" said an older woman.

Luke chuckled. The last time a Rennells approached him, away from the celebration party, the night went on longer than it should have. Although eighteen years older than Ruth, Casey was full on attractive. "It's much better in the East," he turned to face the stadium. What happened three years ago couldn't happen now again. The celebrity gave his eyes no opportunity to explore the woman next to him.

"Do you know why that is?" she asked.

"Never actually thought about it."

"The lights . . ." said Casey as she looked over the Island, "the East is darker at night."

"Ah," he replied as he slipped up, "fair enough."

His eyes weren't where they were suppose to be anymore. Casey was well built. She looked more like an athlete than a detective. The shape of her hips complimented her legs. She held a mug in her hand and the free one had a ring on it . . . a wedding ring?

Luke lost interest as quick as he had found it. Guilt overcame him. He checked to see if anyone witnessed his examination of Mrs. Rennells. Nah, it couldn't be *Rennells* anymore. She belonged to someone, and thank God that person wasn't watching him.

"You're quiet polite," said Casey, with a smile, "you could have almost any girl in the city, but you at least have the decency to leave the married ones alone."

Luke said nothing.

"I like you, Luke," she continued, "I think you're cute, especially your little saying . . . how did it go again? I heard it from one of the guys in the department. 'A woman with no token is a woman not taken.' Cute man. I'm sure Oscar would agree with you."

Was she referring to the Captain of the NCPA?

"Thank you for your service," Luke said, lost for words.

"Look at you being all shy on me."

"I'm –"

"Really, I can see why the girls fall for you," said Casey, "you got the same charm your father had."

Luke froze. By no means was the weather a factor though. He didn't know what got him more. The fact that she knew his father, or the fact that she *knew* his father. Past tense. Did he really want to find out? His wish. Did he still want it to come true?

"Let me tell you about the first case I was involved in," the detective leaned against the railing. "It happened eighteen years ago, when you were only two years old."

The words that flowed from her lips flew over the kid in shock. He listened as she told him arguably every detail of the case she had solved. How she got involved in it. How she met Luke's father and eventually his mother too. They were involved in the case, but they weren't the good guys. She ensured him that that didn't mean his mother didn't love him.

"Bad guys are human too," said Casey, "they have feelings like we do. They care like we do. Love like we do. But don't be deceived, not all of them are like us. Some are inhuman, but portray themselves otherwise . . . until their true colours show."

"Ms. Miller mentioned a man got arrested that night," managed Luke. "Did he –"

"Kill your mother? No . . . your mother was killed by us, the NCPA."

Could she not say that differently? How was death not highlighted red in their dictionary? The cops spoke about it like they saw it daily.

"She was held hostage," Casey continued, "and almost broke free when the man shot and killed his partner, your father."

Luke's parents were actually criminals . . . they deserved to die. Nah –

"No one gets to make that decision, Luke. No one gets to decide who deserves to die or not. Our Force thought they had a chance to take him out, which wasn't the plan, and it backfired. He grabbed your mother and used her as a shield for the bullets."

He deserved to die . . .

Liquor. "Where was I?"

"You were safe inside the building when all this took place," replied Casey. "Your mother loved you more than anything, Luke. She told me your name and entrusted that I would personally keep you safe."

"You're the reason why Ms. Miller has been like a mother to me," stated Luke. "Why Marge taught me to defend myself? She must have been asked to."

"I don't know anything about that, but you sound like you have a point there. I'm more the reason why Captain Den has been showing up every time you are in trouble with the law," she said, "he's been doing me a favor since I moved East. I ensured your mother that you would be kept safe until you were old enough to hear . . . old enough to *understand* the truth." Casey finished her coffee, cold, "And here we are."

"Who was she to you?" Luke asked the million dollar question, "My mother . . ."

"She was a woman who unknowingly helped me solve the case. I just returned the favor," said the detective, "if anything, she has been watching over you in the dark times and the good times, you just didn't know it."

"Like the stars," he smiled, "even though you can't see them in the day, doesn't mean they not watching from the heavens."

Luke's closest friends joined them on the balcony.

"Couldn't have said it *banner* myself . . ." joked Isaac.

"The wish came true," said Marge.

Indeed it did. The final knowledge Luke desired. The knowledge about his parents. Although it hurt to hear of their deaths, to a point that revenge lurked beneath, the comfort of his mother's love covered it. Knowledge that he wasn't abandoned, but loved, all along.

THREE WEEKS LATER

THE HIDDEN GENRE

EPILOGUE

ISAAC BANNER, for the first time in his life, was blindfolded. His girlfriend, Ruth Rennells, slowly pushed him along into an unknown building.

"I hope you haven't forgot about our conversation at the store," said Claude, alongside him, "today will be the start of great things to come."

The blindfolded man was brought to a halt. Ruth slowly revealed the inside of the building to her boyfriend. It all came back to him, the real reason why Claude had visited.

"Only because Elohim saw it fit that way," Isaac had said.

"Without a doubt He was behind it all, because I ignored your raps until that final," Claude had said, "yes, it's true. That final was the game changer. And where I am now is all history, but I had to leave the country to make something happen."

"Tell me about it, this country is filled with secular artists."

"And that's more reason for us to push harder," Claude had said. "How else are they going to hear the Good News? That's why we want you to join us."

"In the competition?"

"Yes, but also in the project Johnny and I are working on. We would be honoured if you joined us, Isaac."

"What kind of project?" he had asked.

Ruth removed the blindfold completely. Isaac was paralyzed with joy. Both their families were amongst the people in attendance. Margarette, Luke, the CBM colleagues and some people they didn't even recognize.

The saying always went about one finding love when one's not looking for it. Isaac had found his love for Ruth early, it was only a matter of time to him. His dream of spreading the Word through music for a living was a dream he chased and chased, but to no avail. No secular label ever got back to him. Then the past revealed itself, upon Luke's return, which kept him too busy to pursue his dream.

Yet, all along hidden in the chaos. He was being prepared. Elohim put him in situations to build the character he needed to handle the pressure of being *amongst* secular artists, not being one.

"We welcome you, our brother," said Claude, who offered a hand to the artist, "to our label . . . C:map Records!"

ACKNOWLEDGEMENTS

Sitting in the audience receiving my thanks would be my one of a kind mother and step pops, who have supported me in more ways than I could have imagined. My grandma, who sent me to the shop to buy her biscuits whenever I needed a break from my writing. My brother, who I still haven't convinced the importance of reading to, hopefully this will change things. My partner, who's patience, extra eyes and support, helped during the writing process. My book art designer, who created an awesome cover! All my managers and colleagues at Bargain Books have played their part as well and many thanks goes to them, those who have left and those working currently. Many other friends and family would be in this audience and I'm grateful for them all, including all those involved in No Greater Treasure Ministry.

Finally, but just as important, a huge thank you to you, the reader, for taking a risk and giving the book a try regardless of me being a new author. This includes all those that maybe bought the book *just* because you know me personally and wanted to support. Yes, you too mommy! Thank you . . .

ABOUT THE AUTHOR

Michael de Oliveira, is a writer of fiction and fantasy. He lives in Cape Town, South Africa with amazing, lovable, and sometimes loud family members. I mean, lovebirds. Oh, as well as a cockatiel or two. He works in a bookshop where he spends his days selling books and his nights writing them. *C. H. H. Ain't Dead: The Hidden Genre* is his debut novel.

www.facebook.com/AuthorMichaeldeOliveira/
fiction.michaeldeoliveira@gmail.com

Made in the USA
Columbia, SC
03 May 2023

15948059R00157